Praise for other Puffin books by Candy Dawson Boyd

◇◇◇

Fall Secrets

"Will strike a responsive chord."   —*Booklist*

Chevrolet Saturdays

"While celebrating the importance of honesty, integrity, and supportive family relationships, Boyd also tries to raise consciousness on racial issues."

—*Kirkus Reviews*

Forever Friends

"Vivid writing so deeply involved and involving that [the reader] has no choice but to live it through."

—*The Reading Teacher*

Other Puffin books
about African—Americans

◇◇◇

Amos Fortune, Free Man	Elizabeth Yates
The Bridges of Summer	Brenda Seabrooke
Charlie Pippin	Candy Dawson Boyd
Chevrolet Saturdays	Candy Dawson Boyd
Fast Sam, Cool Clyde, and Stuff	Walter Dean Myers
Forever Friends	Candy Dawson Boyd
Freedom Songs	Yvette Moore
Growin'	Nikki Grimes
The Hundred Penny Box	Sharon Bell Mathis
Just Like Martin	Ossie Davis
Just My Luck	Emily Moore
Let the Circle Be Unbroken	Mildred D. Taylor
Listen for the Fig Tree	Sharon Bell Mathis
Ludie's Song	Dirlie Herlihy
Marcia	John Steptoe
My Life with Martin Luther King, Jr.	Coretta Scott King
The Road to Memphis	Mildred D. Taylor
Roll of Thunder, Hear My Cry	Mildred D. Taylor
Sidewalk Story	Sharon Bell Mathis
Something to Count On	Emily Moore
Take a Walk in Their Shoes	Glennette Tilley Turner
Teacup Full of Roses	Sharon Bell Mathis
They Had a Dream	Jules Archer
Won't Know 'til I Get There	Walter Dean Myers
The Young Landlords	Walter Dean Myers

A Different Beat

PUFFIN BOOKS
Published by the Penguin Group
Penguin Books USA Inc., 375 Hudson Street,
New York, New York 10014, U.S.A.
Penguin Books Ltd, 27 Wrights Lane, London W8 5TZ, England
Penguin Books Australia Ltd, Ringwood, Victoria, Australia
Penguin Books Canada Ltd, 10 Alcorn Avenue,
Toronto, Ontario, Canada M4V 3B2
Penguin Books (N.Z.) Ltd, 182-190 Wairau Road,
Auckland 10, New Zealand

Penguin Books Ltd, Registered Offices:
Harmondsworth, Middlesex, England

First published in the United States of America by Puffin Books,
1996
1 3 5 7 9 10 8 6 4 2

Copyright © Candy Dawson Boyd, 1996
All rights reserved
Library of Congress Cataloging-in-Publication Data
Boyd, Candy Dawson.
A different beat / Candy Dawson Boyd.
p. cm.
Sequel to: Fall secrets.
Summary: Jessie develops self-esteem as she proves to herself and to
her father that she can succeed both academically and personally at
a performing arts middle school.
ISBN 0-14-036582-6 (pbk.)
[1. Self-esteem—Fiction. 2. Fathers and daughters—Fiction.
3. Acting—Fiction. 4. Schools—Fiction. 5. Afro-Americans—Fiction.]
I. Title.
PZ7.B69157Di 1996 [Fic]—dc20 95-49569 CIP AC

Printed in the United States of America
Set in New Baskerville

A Different Beat

by

CANDY DAWSON BOYD

PUFFIN BOOKS

The doorbell chimed again and again. Jessie jumped, as she woke suddenly from her nap. She dumped her math book on the floor, flung her blanket off, and hurried to the door.

In seconds, she unlocked the door and moved aside as her mother hurried in, followed by her sister, Cass, and Joe, Cass's boyfriend. Glancing up at the darkening sky outside, Jessie flinched as thunder boomed. Cold rain and wind blew in her face.

"Joe, would you please grab those grocery bags for me?" asked Mrs. Williams, sleek and elegant in her burgundy rain slicker and matching hat. "Cass, would you help him with the rest of the packages? I tell you winter is something else. We just finished celebrating Cass's birthday and suddenly the cast party is tonight, and Thanksgiving's next week. How am I ever going to get ready? Not to mention Christmas, Kwanzaa, New Year's Eve, school events, and quarterly taxes? If spring ever arrives, I'll be too exhausted to notice."

As Mrs. Williams fretted, she shed her coat, dropped her hat on a wooden hook, and fixed her eyes on Jessie. "You ate the soup I left you? And took your medicine? Let me feel your forehead. Good, it's cooler."

"I'm fine, Mom. Let me help." Jessie snatched a bag from Cass.

Even in the middle of one of the worst rainstorms in recent years, every hair on her older sister's head was in place. Cass looked, well, just perfect.

Jessie no longer felt the old twang of jealousy inside. Cass's skin was the color of cream. She wore her naturally straight hair long and loose. It fell below her shoulders. "Cass is tougher than she appears to be. Poor Joe, he's learning that the hard way," Jessie thought.

Tall, slender, and perfectly groomed, Cass dumped two shopping bags on the kitchen table. With a slow twirl, she faced her boyfriend. "Joe, there's more in the trunk. And in the backseat. And I need my pom-poms out of your car. Be careful with them. I don't want them wet."

Jessie watched him. Handsome wasn't an adequate

description of Joe. Like Cass used to say, "Joe's so fine, it hurts."

"Sure, Cass, no problem," said Joe, looking as grateful as a puppy to be able to lug groceries, tablecloths, napkins, flowers, pom-poms—and whatever else Cass allowed him to do. He dashed out into the storm.

Jessie grinned, relishing the sight of her sister in action. Joe deserved every ounce of punishment Cass had in store for him for the next seventy-seven years!

"Cass sure has changed," thought Jessie. "She's not the same girl Joe tried to bully into getting a lot closer than she wanted to. Cass doesn't take any stuff off him now. And Joe seems to like it. I'll never understand boys."

"You kids fix yourselves something to eat. I want to take a hot bath and call your father," said Mrs. Williams. "Later I may need you to run down to the bookstore and take him dinner, before we go to the theater." She paused. "I dread this time of year. He works so hard in that darn bookstore, it scares me. Your father is not a young man anymore."

"I'll put in some time at the bookstore, Mom," offered Cass. "So will Joe." Standing in the doorway, loaded down with bags and four red-and-white pom-poms, Joe happily bobbed his head in agreement.

"Me too," said Jessie. "I'll help Dad."

Mrs. Williams nodded, and headed downstairs to the lower level of the house where the bedrooms and bathrooms were.

"Jess, get back on the sofa, under that blanket," ordered Cass. "Joe, help me put all this stuff away. I want to take a nap before we go to Mamatoo's play tonight. So pick me up around 7:00."

Joe nodded eagerly and Jessie had to turn away to keep from laughing out loud. Sometimes life was fair.

Thirty minutes later, the house was quiet. With Joe gone, and Mrs. Williams in a hot bubble bath, a peace settled around the sisters. Jessie bit into the turkey sandwich Cass brought her, watching as her sister filled the bowl in front of her with more hot chicken soup. Feeling a sneeze coming on, Jessie reached for a tissue.

"More chicken soup? Don't we have any split pea or tomato?" she asked.

Cass chuckled. "Research shows that chicken soup relieves nasal and sinus congestion. So drink up, Jess."

"Cass, I'm drowning in chicken soup! I don't care about breathing!"

"Then you may not be well enough to go to school on Monday, or to the play tonight," warned Cass.

Between sneezes, Jessie protested, "No, I have to be there tonight and on Monday I have to see Mrs. Grant. I mean I . . ."

Cass put her hand out and held Jessie's. With skin the color of double chocolate brownies, and naturally nappy hair, Jessie did not physically resemble Cass at all. But they were full-blooded sisters.

"I still feel like I have to see Mrs. Grant. Face to face. I want her to see me and I want to see her. She may still look at me and see a dark, dumb, ugly girl who couldn't possibly be your younger sister. But I can't believe that's who I am. I don't want to ever think that part of me was too scared to see her." Jessie blew her nose.

"I'm so proud of you. I'll be there with you. I can't believe that Mrs. Grant was once my favorite teacher," Cass said.

Jessie thought out loud. "Sometimes I wish I hadn't heard what I did. It was two years ago, but when I close my eyes, I can see and hear every single thing. It was the worst day of my life, Cass. I thought Mrs. Grant liked me. I really did. I loved her."

Cass murmured, "I know you did, Jess. You were so good to her."

Memories skipped through Jessie's mind. When Mrs. Grant had put her in charge of the classroom library, Jessie had written her a thank you note on her mother's lavender notepaper. Mrs. Grant had put it up on the small bulletin board by her desk.

On Mrs. Grant's birthday, Jessie had saved her money and bought a fancy birthday card. Mrs. Grant had written her a thank you note on a card with yellow roses on the front. That card lay in a box of special treasures under Jessie's bed.

Tears brimmed in Jessie's eyes.

"I'm so sorry, Jess," said Cass softly. "I feel responsible."

"You're not responsible for what Mrs. Grant did! It's not your fault that she believes that light-skinned black girls with straight hair are prettier and smarter than me. Like you told me, we have to stand up for ourselves. We can't let people stick us in the box they want us to fit into," said Jessie.

"I know," cried Cass. "But I'm your big sister and I should have been able to help you."

Jessie dried her eyes. Imitating their grandmother, Mamatoo, she stood up and said, "Enough! Stop blaming yourself. Want me to hug you and give you my cold? Then you could give it to Joe. How's that for a plan?"

"I'll take my chances," said Cass, hugging her. "Did you get your homework done? I'm not trying to hassle you, but Dad's on a rampage."

"Would Dad really make me leave OPA and go to that school-of-the-dead Milton Middle School? Tell me the truth, Cass."

"Come on, Jess. You know he will. If you don't get good grades this term, you can kiss Oakland Performing Arts Middle School good-bye."

Jessie bit her lip. "I thought going to OPA would be a dream come true. I mean, it is, but there's so much work to do. Now I've got Dad on my back and that crazy girl Addie Mae Cooper!"

"Let me see if I can get this right, there are three other girls in your Home Base group."

"Score one," said Jessie, sipping soup.

Cass grinned. "Hit it! Maria Hernandez. Julie Stone. And Addie Mae Cooper."

"Score two, three, and four!"

With a clap of her hands, Cass continued. "Maria is studying piano. Julie loves the violin and her cat, Toby. Addie Mae is a dancer, but that isn't her real name. I can't remember the rest."

"Score five, six, seven and a half."

"So, remind me, Jess."

"If that wacky girl changes her name one more time, I'll go crazy! First she called herself Obidie, a female Nigerian name that means 'father's beloved child'. Then she gets angry about something and changes her name to Mkiwa. That means something about being orphaned. Who knows what her new African name will be? Her real name should be 'Miss Mouth!' She's always trying to talk and act so super black," sputtered Jessie. "Anyway, forget her. She's not worth my time."

"I can tell she's not on your list of favorites. You better hit those books, Jess. Or I'll pour you another bowl of chicken soup."

The sisters giggled. Jessie snuggled under the blanket on the sofa and picked up her math homework. Her head spun like the blades on a helicopter. Her stomach hurt, but it wasn't from her cold.

Heavy rain pelted the windows and sliding doors. From the bare hillside, empty of trees, the northern California Bay Area spread out before her. She could see the city of Berkeley, part of Oakland, and the Bay Bridge.

Last year, the fire in the hills had cleared the land below their home. She could see how close to the house the fire had come. Right up to the deck.

When Jessie checked the clock, almost fifteen minutes had passed. She had hours of homework and a big math test coming up. Determined, Jessie tried to focus on her homework, but the math problems just kept swimming around in her head.

❖❖❖

When the front door opened it gave Jessie a start. Mamatoo, her maternal grandmother, shook the rain off. Jessie hadn't heard the familiar sputtering sound of Mamatoo's Volkswagen.

"There's my girl! How's that cold?" Mamatoo's husky voice reached across the living room like a hug.

"Oh! I'm so glad to see you. How did dress rehearsal go?" asked Jessie. "Does the new blocking for the last part of Act Two work?"

"Fine. Changing the way Cheryl moved around Maurice and repositioning the couch made all the difference in the world. Opening night tonight. I had to take a break and come home. What's up?" Mamatoo settled herself on the side of the sofa, the folds of her caftan spread around her like iridescent peacock feathers. Her matching head wrap glowed against her fair skin.

Jessie swallowed. The truth flowed out, words tumbling over each other. "Mamatoo, I don't want to see Mrs. Grant. Not ever again! I'm scared. I don't believe that Mrs. Grant is really sorry for what she said."

Jessie waited for her grandmother to reassure her. But Mamatoo simply sat there staring out at the bleak, fire-scarred Berkeley hills.

"Are you ashamed of me for feeling like this?" murmured Jessie.

"I can't imagine being ashamed of you for sharing your honest feelings. Heavens, child, I'd be afraid to face a teacher I once loved and trusted who betrayed everything I felt for her."

Jessie rested her head on Mamatoo's shoulder. She closed her eyes. She could see Mrs. Grant in the hallway after school, talking to a teacher friend. Neither one realized that Jessie had returned to get her book bag. The echo of Mrs. Grant's words reverberated in her head.

Each word had hit Jessie like a slap in the face: "I can't believe the Williams girls are sisters. Cassandra was one of the prettiest black girls I have ever taught, and one of the smartest. That beautiful long, glossy hair, and white skin. It's hard to believe that Jessie is her sister. She's so dark and plain. Not even that smart—such a disappointment after Cassandra." Tears had streamed down Jessie's cheeks.

Jessie had kept that painful secret for two years and only a few weeks ago had told her family.

"I know that all of you went back to my elementary school and demanded an apology from Mrs. Grant," said Jessie.

"Honey, your daddy wanted to sue the school district. We reluctantly settled for an apology—one delivered by that woman to you face-to-face." Mamatoo's eyes were fixed on the stark trees. "That woman lied. She denied every word you said."

"I'm afraid, Mamatoo," Jessie confessed again.

"Of what, Jessie? Now, think long and hard. What's got you so frightened? Is there some part of what that woman said that you believe?" Mamatoo focused her wide brown eyes on her granddaughter.

Jessie searched her heart. It would take something very special to recover from the damage done that day. And it would take even more to make up for all the years of feeling like the plain, ugly one when compared to Cass.

Even her own father made her feel that way. As hard as she tried, Jessie couldn't forget she had never been her father's favorite—not even a close second. For Dad, Cass was first, second, and third.

Her father was proud of his oldest daughter's decision to become a pediatrician. Jessie knew that her own goal of becoming a great actress didn't impress him one bit. In fact, Dad barely tolerated her attending OPA. He had said: At least all B grades, or no OPA. Dad delivered simple, potent threats.

"Oh, Mamatoo," said Jessie. "I know I'm not dumb.

Shoot, I've been able to survive two months at OPA. Just getting accepted there was a big deal! And my drama teacher, Mr. Reynolds, says I have real talent as an actress."

"Humph. I told you that years ago. So we can eliminate Jessie Williams the Dumb Girl. What about the rest?" Mamatoo shifted her weight, leaning back as she held her granddaughter. She kicked off her shoes and folded her legs beneath her.

"Mamatoo, do you want some tea? I'll make you a cup."

"Don't you move one inch! Now, answer me," demanded Mamatoo.

Settling back, Jess sighed. "I don't feel pretty like Cass. But don't tell the rest of the family, Mamatoo. I don't want them telling me that being dark with hair that needs straightening is fine."

Mamatoo sighed. "Well, you told the sweet truth there. You've got to feel it in your heart. Like they say, 'Walk your talk.' Jessie, I believe that you are one of the most beautiful, intelligent, gifted young women I've ever known. Now, part of my belief can be directly attributed to the fact that you are my granddaughter. But—"

"Do I believe that what Mrs. Grant said about me is true?" Jessie asked.

"I'm waiting for an honest answer."

The hush in the room settled around Jessie. Mamatoo had asked a hard, painful question. Jessie wasn't sure she could tell her grandmother the truth. She wasn't even sure she knew what the whole truth was. After the silence stretched into minutes, Mamatoo stood up.

"Well, let's put that on the back burner for now. We've got an opening night!" she said. "Come on downstairs with me—bring your old, ratty blanket. You can figure out your life while I do my yoga."

Jessie followed her grandmother downstairs, trailing the soft blue blanket behind her. One quick peek into the bedroom she shared with her sister showed that Cass was napping. Her mom was on the phone with her dad.

Mamatoo's apartment looked as if it had been waiting for her to return. A bouquet of rich yellow chrysanthemums and daisies decorated a small round table in the dining area. The clock hummed. In a few moments, subdued light from lamps and candles warmed the room, while the cold rain continued to pummel the windows outside.

Jessie walked around the large room. Her grandfather, Mom's father, had died three years ago. The best thing in the world happened when Mom had insisted that her mother move in with them and occupy the attached apartment. Of course, feisty Mamatoo insisted on paying her own rent and utilities.

Of all Jessie's grandparents, Mamatoo was her absolute favorite. The only time Jessie saw her paternal grandparents was during the holidays. They were nice, but ordinary. Nobody could match her Mamatoo!

Finding her own special corner of the couch was easy

for Jessie. Thinking about Mrs. Grant wasn't. Snuggled, warm and safe, Jessie wondered what it would take to be able to gaze at herself in a mirror and smile. "If I had not believed her," she thought, "I could have spoken right up to her! Right then and there! Well, I'm going to get my chance real soon. I hope I can do it. What if I can't?"

The logs shifted, shooting sparks up the chimney. Jessie's grandmother had finished her yoga, made the fire, bathed, and was sipping a cup of mint tea.

"Jessie, you must tell the truth that is in your heart. Do you believe what Mrs. Grant said about you?"

Mamatoo would sit there until spring, waiting for even a shred of an honest response.

"No, I don't believe all of it. I don't think I'm ugly, just not pretty. Well, nothing special. I'm smart. I may not be as fast as Cass in some areas. But like you say, 'You can't be a good, stupid actress.' "

That remark tickled them.

Mamatoo's wide smile narrowed. Her eyes darkened. Her eyebrows, like black ink strokes, knitted together. "So are you going to face Mrs. Grant in less than forty-eight hours or not, Jessie Williams? You'll be surrounded by your family."

Jessie squirmed. "I want to be able to stand in front of Mrs. Grant and hear her apologize. But, Mamatoo, is an apology a real apology if the person isn't sincere? Mrs. Grant denied saying what she did. So the only reason she's apologizing is because she has to. I don't know if I really want to go 'through all of this just for that.' "

Her grandmother stood up. "Perhaps you need to spend more time thinking about it. I believe that despite your fears, you need to face her, but this is your call, Jess. Not mine or your parents' or your sister's. Your choice."

"You're right, Mamatoo."

"I need to rest for a while. Are you well enough to make opening night?"

Jessie's eyes widened. "You bet I am! I've never missed one of your opening nights! I'd better go upstairs and help get everything ready for the cast party."

◇◇◇

That night, Jessie and most of her family went to see the play Mamatoo's repertory company was performing. Her father had called to say that he would be working late. A large shipment of books had come in and he had to unpack and inventory them. But he would be home for the cast party after the performance.

When the curtain fell at the end of the final act, Jessie clapped until her palms hurt. So did the rest of the audience in the packed theater. The cast received standing ovations for all five curtain calls. Jessie thought that her grandmother looked splendid on the small stage. As artistic director, Mamatoo carried a great deal of the responsibility for the success or failure of the company. The enthusiastic applause signaled that the season was off to a great start.

At the cast party, Jessie listened to the actresses and actors talk about the play. She had spent most of her life around theater people. She noticed that even the actors with little roles smiled and laughed.

"Like Mamatoo says, a successful play requires the best from everyone. There are no small parts, only small actors," she thought.

Jessie herself would be performing a small part as Harriet Tubman's younger sister in the Winter Festival play at OPA. Not the part she had hoped to get, but at least she'd be in the play. Getting called back to audition for the chorus had been an unexpected surprise. The chorus was an important, distinctive part of the play.

As the evening went on, Jessie lent a hand in the kitchen. She replenished the buffet. Laughter and conversation flowed freely. Eventually, though, the party wound down.

Standing by the stereo, lost in her thoughts, Jessie was unaware that her father had moved next to her. She jumped when he touched her arm. Dad and Cass resembled one another very much. But there was no welcome on her father's face. Behind his glasses, his eyes were hard.

"Hi, Dad. The play was wonderful. The theater was packed and people wouldn't stop clapping! I know the reviews are going to be raves," she said.

"Good." Mr. Williams took a sip of punch. "Jessie, your mother told me you offered to help me at the bookstore during the holiday season. With Cass and Joe, I should be fine. Your first and only priority is your studies."

"Yeah, Dad."

"Jess, I realize that this acting bug you've got is very important to you. But the theater is one of the toughest games in town. Being black doesn't help you. You have to be employable," he said.

The dark circles under his eyes seemed to get darker every day, a sure sign that he wasn't getting enough rest. Dad removed his glasses and pinched the bridge of his nose.

"I could always fit in some work at the bookstore. I know how to do everything there," Jessie offered, trying to lighten the mood.

"Daughter, this is not a joking matter. The only A's you

got at midsemester were in Improvisation and Reader's Theater. A B⁻ in science and in math is not acceptable," he said, his voice low, but firm. "If your grades aren't all B's or better at the end of this term, I am going to have to think seriously about sending you to Milton Middle School. It's a solid academic school."

"Dad, I'll die if I have to leave OPA. I love it there. I auditioned with hundreds of other kids to just get in. And I made it! All I need is time to adjust. I'm a preadolescent facing enormous changes."

"Have you been listening to those silly talk shows? 'Time to adjust!' " He rolled his eyes. "Jessie, you've got one term, *this* term, to get at least straight B's. Cass got straight A's from the beginning. She understands the value of a strong, academic education. Not that frivolous nonsense like acting."

Jessie cringed. "Dad's favorite pastime," she thought, "comparing me to Cass—and putting down actors and acting."

"I'm me, Dad. I'm not Cass," she said, tugging at one of the gold earrings Cass had given her. "And I *am* an actress."

Mr. Williams's mouth tightened. "I know that. I know you are different from your sister. Aren't you listening to me, Jessie? It's a tough world out there. Acting won't cut it. Every actor at this party has at least one other job so they can eat! I don't want you living like that."

Jessie fumed. There was no way she was going to leave

OPA. It had taken her months of grueling work to win a place as an OPA student-artist. If Dad made her leave OPA, she didn't know what she would do.

"Dad, my grades will be good. I need to go help Mom clean up."

"We'll let it drop for now, Jessie, but your number one job is to get good grades. Remember that."

"I sure will, Dad." Jessie faked an obedient-daughter-who-will-do-everything-her-father-says smile and got away as fast as she could.

◇◇◇

By Sunday afternoon, Jessie was worn out. Cass was out with Joe, so the bedroom she shared with her sister provided a safe hideout.

Jessie stared out the bedroom window at the relentless storm. Heavy rainstorms roaring in, one after the other, signaled winter in this part of California. Jessie shook her head. Rains like this could cause mud slides. After the fire last November, mud slides spelled potential disaster.

Jessie could still envision the fire burning around her. She could hear the helicopters whirling above and people screaming. How could a fire consume more than five hundred homes? Scorch thousands of acres of wooded land? Kill so many people? And ruin the lives of thousands more? Only Dad's courage and luck had saved their house. Mom's courage and luck had saved their lives.

"Courage. That's what my family has. Real courage. I

have courage, too. But what do I say to Mrs. Grant? How do I act?" Jessie murmured to the storm outside. It was too late to back out now.

Minutes later Jessie was standing at the far end of the downstairs hall, facing the door to Mamatoo's apartment. She took a deep breath and pushed the buzzer four times, one long and three short, her special code. The door swung open.

"I've been waiting for you." Mamatoo smiled.

"Mamatoo, you've got to help me. I don't know what to do or say tomorrow at the meeting." Jessie flopped on the sofa. "I'm sorry. Congratulations on the reviews."

"Thank you. Now, let's make you a hit. We're actresses. Let's try some scenarios."

Jessie leaped up. "Mamatoo, that's absolutely, one thousand percent brilliant! Why didn't I think of that?"

"Never mind. Let's get to work. How shall we set this up?"

"You be Mrs. Grant. I'll be me."

"I certainly hope so," chuckled her grandmother, moving two of the chairs at the dining room table over to the living room area.

"Will the principal be there?" wondered Jessie. "I bet he will. So we've got the principal, Mrs. Grant, me, you, Dad, Mom, and Cass."

"That's a roomful of people!" said Mamatoo.

"What if I get angry?" asked Jessie.

"Your temper is a problem. All right, Miss What If, let's

play it out." Mamatoo sat down in a chair and folded her hands. "Lay the scene out, child, you know how."

"We get to the school. We get out of the car and walk into the school. I hold Cass's hand and yours. We walk to the office. The principal comes out and invites us in. We walk in. Should I go first or last?" Jessie wrung her hands.

"Relax, Jessie. Don't sweat the small stuff. Just concentrate on what makes you feel comfortable." Mamatoo crossed her legs. "Now, use that fine brain of yours."

Jessie concentrated. "I want to go in between you and Dad with Mom and Cass behind me. So, we walk into the principal's office." Suddenly, Jessie panicked. "What am I wearing? What am I going to wear?" The expression on her grandmother's face calmed her back down. "I need to wear whatever makes me feel comfortable. Right?"

Mamatoo smiled her approval. "Absolutely one thousand percent brilliant."

"Then I'll wear the beautiful gold hoop earrings Cass gave me. And my good-luck T-shirt under the red pullover sweater you got me for my birthday. Blue jeans and my new boots."

"Good! Keep working. Now, what are you going to say in your comfortable clothes?"

Jessie marched back and forth. "We walk in and sit down. The principal has to say something polite. Then Mrs. Grant speaks. I sit there. We get up and leave. It's all over. Sounds like a plan to me."

"Jessie Williams, stop procrastinating! There's no sense even going if that's what happens. What happened to 'What if I get angry'? Let's play that scene. I'm the principal, now."

"OK."

Mamatoo rustled in the chair. Then she settled down and folded her hands again. A bright, fake smile lit her face. She was the principal.

"Thank you for coming. I know that this is an awkward time for all of us. But I'm sure that we can handle this in a cooperative, professional way. Now, Jessie, I understand that you believe that Mrs. Grant said some things two years ago that upset you. Although Mrs. Grant has no memory of this incident, she certainly does not want to see you upset. Isn't that right, Mrs. Grant?"

A surge of hot anger streaked up Jessie's spine. Furious, she whirled around.

"Wait a minute! I didn't make this up! Why would I lie? She did tell the other teacher I was slow. She said she didn't expect much from me. You said that, Mrs. Grant! You said that I wasn't pretty like Cass. You said I was dark-skinned and funny-looking!"

Still in the role of the school principal, Mamatoo held her hands out in a conciliatory gesture.

"Now, now, there's no need to get emotional about this, Jessie. Let's stay calm. I think that Mrs. Grant has something to say."

Mamatoo rearranged her posture. Her face closed up

like a crammed suitcase. Jessie watched her grandmother shift her weight and become Mrs. Grant.

"Jessie, if I said or did anything that hurt you, I am sorry. You were one of my best students. I understand that you are doing well in middle school. I wish you much success."

Jessie forgot that Mamatoo was playing the part of Mrs. Grant. Her hot anger bubbled out again. "That's no real apology! You said those things about me! And you know you did! I want a real apology!"

"Jessie, you always had a tendency to be overly dramatic. I have to get back to my class." Mamatoo, as Mrs. Grant, got up and walked toward the kitchen.

The room was quiet except for the sound of wood burning in the fireplace. Absently Jessie reached for an oatmeal cookie from the plateful Mamatoo had set out.

"I'll probably be too scared to say a thing," said Jessie.

"Then let's play that one out." Mamatoo walked back and took her chair. "Now, from the top. We're in the office. The principal has delivered his 'Be nice' speech. Mrs. Grant has just given her specious excuse for a genuine apology. What happens next?"

"I'll cry or mumble something stupid."

"Do that, then. I'll give you a different apology from Mrs. Grant. Ready? Here it is," directed her grandmother.

Mamatoo shook out her arms. Then she tilted her head and stared at Jessie. "I am glad to see you, Jessie, and your family. I hope that we can resolve this and put it behind us. Jessie, I know what you think you heard me say. I can't imagine saying anything like that about a student of mine. If I ever said anything that you somehow interpreted as being negative, I certainly regret that."

Mamatoo leaned forward in the chair. She looked so sincere and honest.

Jessie bowed her head. Staring at her hands, she said, in a low voice, "Let's go, Dad."

With a gentle hand, Mamatoo squeezed her granddaughter's shoulder. The she got up and put the teakettle on. She added more cookies to the plate on the table.

Jessie held her head in her hands.

"Mamatoo, what am I going to do? I can't explode like a bomb or mumble and run like a scared chicken! I wish I was braver. Even bold like Addie Mae Cooper. She wouldn't have a problem facing Mrs. Grant. Cooper could take down a tank," exclaimed Jessie. "I can't believe I'm sitting here wishing I was Cooper. I must be desperate."

"Jess, you have such extreme emotions about that girl. Never mind her. We have big fish to fry, whale-sized fish. At least you have two options you didn't have before." The teasing edge in her voice made Jessie look up and smile.

"And I know what to wear," said Jessie. Her smile vanished. "I just wish I knew what to say. I wish tomorrow was over."

"In a little more than twenty-four hours it will be. Take this tray," said Mamatoo. "We need some nourishment. That was hard work."

◇◇◇

By the time Jessie crawled into bed that night, the rain had finally stopped.

"Sleep well, Jess," said Cass from her bed across the room. "Don't worry about tomorrow. We'll all be there with you."

"Thanks, Cass."

Jessie squinted her eyes together. In her mind she saw Mrs. Grant—tall and big-boned, with glasses and short, curly hair. Her hands were huge. Jess shivered and scrunched into a ball.

With the covers pulled up and tucked around her, she felt like a caterpillar in a cocoon. Warm air from the vent overhead blew quietly.

Jessie turned to face the wall. "Even if I see Mrs. Grant, what will she say? What will I say? What's going to happen tomorrow? Please God, please make it all right."

Monday morning roared in like a freight train. Jessie examined her reflection in the bathroom mirror. Sometimes she forgot that only weeks ago she had messed up and dyed her hair red. Chili-pepper red. Miss Mouth—Addie Mae Cooper—took pleasure in comparing her to a fire engine. It would take at least three more months before her dyed hair grew out, unless she got it cut super short.

Jessie spoke to her mirror image, "That's something I haven't thought about. Dad would be furious if I cut my hair off. But how long can I go around looking like this?"

Her planned outfit felt fine—comfortable and secure. A tinge of warmth filled Jessie when she touched the earrings from Cass. Jessie gathered her books and went upstairs. The meeting with Mrs. Grant loomed like a mythical monster, waiting for her at the end of the school day.

"Breakfast, Jess?" asked Cass. "How's the cold?"

"No thanks, I'm not hungry. My head feels like there's a pillow stuffed inside, but other than that and the conference after school, I couldn't be better," said Jess, taking the glass of milk and the banana Cass handed her.

Mrs. Williams came up to the kitchen. In her tailored suit and blouse, she looked glamorous.

"How could Mamatoo ever say that I'd grow up to look like Mom? No way," Jessie thought.

"So here are my girls. Are you two feeling all right? Cass, put your schedule for the week on the refrigerator door. Jess, I'll pick you up right after school," said Mom, "Now, let's get a move on. We're running late."

The doorbell rang.

Cass grabbed her coat and book bag. "It's Joe. See you after school, Jess. Hang tough today."

The ride to school with her mother was usually a chatty time. Today, Jessie couldn't think of anything to say. Her throat felt as clogged as her head. The trip from the Berkeley hills down to the flatlands was desolate this Monday morning.

Trees, stripped of most of their leaves by the rainstorm,

stood like defeated soldiers. Thick sheets of dark plastic covered the barren hills. Bereft of windows, doors, and walls, just the brick shells of fireplaces were all that remained of hundreds of homes. The sight of the fireplaces standing alone still stung.

Jessie watched the expert way her mother maneuvered the car around the sharp curves and corkscrew twists in the road, just as she had driven them through the heart of the fire to safety that terrible Sunday afternoon. Her father had stayed behind at the house to fight the fire. "Courage—and luck," remembered Jessie.

When they finally reached OPA, Jessie headed for the sixth-grade wing, where her Home Base was. The sight of the hallway walls decorated with huge murals of dancers, musicians, singers, actors, and artists of all kinds delighted her.

One sharp right, past the library, and she was in Academic House A, heading for Room 114. Briefly, Jessie stopped at her locker, shed her coat, and dumped some books.

Mr. Reynolds, her Home Base, drama, and humanities teacher, stood by the classroom door. Jessie fell into the rapidly moving stream of fellow sixth graders.

"Good morning, Miss Williams. How's that cold of yours?" he asked, his voice full and rich.

"Better, thank you, Mr. Reynolds." Jessie tried to smile.

"I can't quite believe that smile of yours—Good morning, Miss Hawkins—You're too good an actress, Jessie, and that smile is artificial—Good morning, Mr. Randall and Miss Schenberg," he said.

Jessie stared into his dark face. "This is a hard day for me, Mr. Reynolds."

He smiled slowly. "Can you make it a good day?"

"I'm going to do my best."

"That's what I want to hear, Miss Williams."

"Yes, sir."

Jessie spotted her cluster, the Fours, near the long bank of windows. No Addie Mae Cooper, as usual. She typically flew in at the last minute. Maria Hernandez and Julie Stone were deep in conversation. For the rest of sixth grade, she'd spend Home Base with these girls.

Julie greeted her. "Jessie! We're trying to figure out how to keep our group project going at Evergreen and keep up with the rest of our—"

"Our do-or-die responsibilities," interrupted Maria, rolling her eyes and running her hands through her rich black hair. "Jessie and I are under the same pressures. We either get top grades or our fathers make us transfer to a regular middle school where we can learn what we 'should.' "

"And I didn't even finish all of my homework!" Jessie confessed. "I've been too worried about the meeting with my old teacher, Mrs. Grant." Jessie glanced at Maria. "My dad will send me straight to jail, meaning Milton Middle School—and I won't get to pass Go or collect my two hundred dollars."

Julie pantomimed playing a violin, her instrument. "My heart is bleeding for you two."

It made Jessie happy to see Julie joking. Her family had lost their home and all of their belongings in the fire. Living in a tiny, cramped apartment had to be difficult. But the Fours had pulled together to help Julie.

"Julie, how's Toby?" asked Jessie.

At the mention of her cat's name, Julie's eyes shone. Framed by light red hair, her freckled, pale face glowed.

"He's wonderful. Having my cat back is the only thing that makes me feel like I have a real home left. I love Toby more than anything. Except my violin," Julie said. "Thanks, Jess, for everything."

"What do you mean, 'Thanks, Jess, for everything'?" declared a voice from behind them. "I helped. So did Maria. Miss Jessie Williams didn't pull that miracle off by herself." The voice alone made Jessie bristle.

With a thud, Addie Mae Cooper dumped her book bag on the floor and eased into her seat.

Maria spoke up. "Cooper, come on. You know what Julie meant. Stop complaining."

Clenching her teeth, Jessie struggled to keep her temper under control. Addie Mae Cooper had on her Monday protest costume: a red, black, and green "Malcolm X Lives Forever!" sweatshirt, beaded African jewelry, rows of political buttons, and combat-fatigue jeans. Her straight hair hung in long braids. Cooper was light-skinned like Cass and Dad.

"What is she trying to prove? How black she is? I wish she would just be herself and stop acting like she's some great freedom fighter," Jessie thought.

Cooper tapped her fingers on the desk. "No big deal, Maria. I was just making a point. Right, Jess? No bad feelings?"

Swallowing her anger, Jessie nodded.

Julie continued, "Anyway, Toby is fine. Thanks to everyone in the world. But, Daddy met with the lawyer this weekend about the insurance company settlement. If we don't get the money we're owed soon, I don't know what's going to happen." Julie's eyes darkened. "My folks have started fighting again."

"It'll work out, Julie. Maybe that should be our next project: exposing insurance companies who aren't being fair," suggested Maria, surveying the group.

Cooper shook her head. "Would take too much time. I have to make it to the first line in the dance troupe. That means hours of practice."

Jessie's words burst out before she could stop them. "Addie Mae, don't you ever think about anything but yourself? You. You. You. I'm sick and tired of you."

"I don't want you calling me Addie Mae. You hear me?" snapped Cooper.

The fragile truce between the two girls snapped. Jessie returned the girl's glare.

"You really think you can be a dancer like Judith Jamison? Girl, you have to be fooling yourself," taunted Jessie.

She knew that the famous African-American dancer was Cooper's idol.

"Yeah? And what about you? Playing bit parts as old women isn't going to get you too far as an actress!" The last words came out with a sneer.

The other two Fours glared at them.

"Stop this," interrupted Maria. "Listen, I have to get a good grade out of this class. I don't know what the problem is with you two, but I have to be selfish right now." "Cooper, what *do* you want to be called?"

"Yes, Miss Cooper, please let all of us know." The sharp tone of Mr. Reynolds's voice made the four girls flinch. Jessie wanted to disappear under the table. "My temper is always getting me into trouble," she thought. "I'd better watch it this afternoon with Mrs. Grant."

"We're all waiting, Miss Cooper," said Mr. Reynolds.

Cooper stood up and faced her teacher. "Mr. Reynolds, I sincerely request permission to move to another group. I can't work with Jessie Williams. We just don't get along."

The whole class shifted its attention to the teacher, waiting for his response.

Mr. Reynolds leaned against the edge of his desk. Jessie expected to see some sign of anger or annoyance on his face. But there wasn't any.

"Maria and Julie, what would you suggest as a wise course of action here?" he asked.

The girls looked at each other and shrugged their shoulders.

"Jessie, do you have a suggestion?" he asked.

All eyes were on her.

Biting her lip, Jessie struggled to respond. Cooper looked like Cass. Between the attention Cass had always gotten from their father and the memory of Mrs. Grant's words, Jessie struggled with the image of light-skinned black girls. Jessie knew the reality that being light-skinned with "good" hair—like whites—meant being pretty, not only to a lot of whites, but to many black people, too, including boys.

"There's something about Cooper I don't trust," she thought. "It's like she can have her cake and eat it too. Be light and still act like the kind of black, into-her-people kid Dad wants me to be. Dad would love to have Cooper as his daughter. She knows a thousand times more than I do about black history and identifies with every black cause in the world. But I can't tell Mr. Reynolds any of this."

"Mr. Reynolds, we don't get along. We try, but it doesn't work," said Jessie, avoiding everyone's eyes.

"You know the rule." Mr. Reynolds spoke calmly, addressing the Fours. "The groups Fate dealt you when you counted off in September are the groups you learn to live with until June. I haven't changed that rule in eight years, despite some very difficult students. So, Miss

Williams and Miss Cooper, you have an extra special project now."

Jessie jumped up. "Oh, please, Mr. Reynolds, I can't take another assignment. I'm buried in assignments!"

Cooper interrupted. "Me too! Look, Mr. Reynolds, we'll work this out some way. Honestly, we don't need a special project. Please!"

Mr. Reynolds strolled to the windows. The class monitored each step. "Well, it appears that I have found something that the two of you can agree on."

"Mr. Reynolds, I promise." Cooper frantically looked to Jessie, who bobbed her head in agreement. "See, we promise, Jessie and me, that there will be no more problems."

Their teacher shook his head.

"Miss Cooper, what makes OPA so unique? The faculty here takes talent and creates the future artists of this country. But we do more. We provide a demanding academic program and we maintain an environment where young people of all races, religions, ethnic groups, talents, and personalities learn how to be members of a community."

"We know that, Mr. Reynolds, and our group will be the best community you ever saw," said Jessie, looking at Cooper.

"The best," Cooper echoed.

"It takes more than words to make a promise," said Mr. Reynolds. "Miss Williams and Miss Cooper, you will work together on a project that combines your gifts—dancing and acting. You will present and share this project with the class the week before the Winter Festival. I expect you to keep personal journals which I will read and respond to. Now let's take attendance and get this Monday going." Turning away from them, he said, "End of discussion."

Deflated, Jessie and Cooper were unable to look at one another. Their teacher started the roll. Hushed voices answered.

"Addie Mae Cooper?" he asked.

"Mr. Reynolds, I prefer that you call me Chuki, which is pronounced 'Choo-kee'. The stress is on the first syllable. It is Kiswahili for 'born when there was animosity.'"

Without blinking an eye, he said, "I see. Just to keep the record straight, this is your third name change, Miss Cooper?"

Cooper gulped. "Right, Mr. Reynolds."

"Thank you," he said. "Chuki Cooper?"

The girl's face was set in concrete. "Present."

When the period ended, the Fours gathered up their book bags silently.

Exasperated, Maria suddenly exclaimed, "I can't believe it, Cooper, another name!"

Julie took up the thread, "When I finally got your African names right, you wanted to be called Cooper. Then you told us about your real name, how you were named after your relative, Addie Mae Collins, who was one of the four little girls killed in Birmingham, Mississippi. A racist white man bombed an African-American church during Sunday school. He killed them. See? I remember every word you said."

"You sure do," admitted Cooper. "Except that it was Alabama, not Mississippi," she added sarcastically.

Maria swung around. Her black eyes blazed, but her voice remained cool. "Listen, Cooper—I mean, Chuki—I have my future as a pianist and Jessie has hers as an actress, riding on the grades we get. You don't have a father breathing down your neck like we do. You don't have somebody who thinks that what you want to do with your life is silly."

Cooper confronted Maria. "You don't know anything about my father, Maria! So shut up!"

Julie stepped in between the two of them. "Chuki, we know he's not the dad you said he was. You told us about the divorce and how you hardly see him anymore. Maria's not trying to upset you. She's just worried. We all have problems."

Jessie remained silent. Figuring out Cooper was impossible! The very thought of working together, just the two of them, was unbelievable. Mr. Reynolds must be nuts!

"I'll handle my problems by myself," Cooper stated. "I can name myself anything I choose. Mr. Reynolds respects my right to freedom of speech. My name is Chuki. That's what I want to be called." She stomped out.

"I'm sorry," Jessie said to Maria and Julie. "If I had controlled my temper, none of this would have happened."

Julie let out a deep sigh. "Whatever's going on between you and Cooper is a long way from getting better. Let's meet this afternoon and figure out what to do about our Home Base project at Evergreen. We've got to think of something more exciting than just going over there and playing music, dancing, and reciting poetry to those nice old people."

They trudged out of the room.

Julie crinkled her nose. "What are the two of you going to do for the special project?"

Jessie wanted to cry. "I don't know. I wish I had kept my big mouth shut and just ignored her."

"No time for wishes. Wishes and fishes." Julie started to giggle. "Fishy wishes."

Maria joined in, giggling, "Fishes and wishes. Fishy wishes. Wishy fishes."

The two of them laughed so hard they had to hold one another up. Jessie didn't find any humor in her predicament or their silliness.

Gasping, Julie panted, "Sorry, Jess. But what *are* you and Cooper going to do for a joint project?"

"I don't have a clue," reiterated Jessie. "I can't deal with this now. I've just got to make it through the day without creating more trouble for myself." Jessie lowered her eyes and walked down the hallway, alone.

"Jessie! Jessie! Wait up!" That voice made her stop in mid-step. She turned around. There he was with those sweet eyes, skin like golden honey, stretched over a tall, muscular frame, and a face that was all sharp angles. Jamar Lewis. It was hard for Jessie to believe that only a few weeks ago the two of them had danced together seven times. Five fast dances and two slow ones.

"What a dummy I was to think that the back-to-school dance would be terrible," thought Jessie. "If it hadn't been for Cass, I never would have gone. She helped me look so pretty."

"Jess, how are you doing?" Jamar asked, out of breath. "I'll walk you to class."

"Thanks. I'm OK. What about you?" The words came out all wrong.

Jamar stopped. He looked hurt. "What's the matter?" he asked. "I thought we were supposed to be friends."

Jessie wanted to yell at him. Why didn't Mr. Jamar Lewis, a seventh-grader and fall-down-fine boy realize that she had trouble uttering words longer than two syllables in his presence? "Doesn't he know that every girl in sixth and seventh grade adores him? Why does he like me?" she asked herself silently.

Jessie took a deep breath, from the gut, the way Mamatoo had taught her. Slowly, she exhaled.

"I'm sorry, Jamar. I lost my temper again this morning—Cooper and I got into it in Home Base. Mr. Reynolds won't let us change groups. He's making us work on a special project together. And after school I have that conference with Mrs. Grant I told you about." The words poured out.

"Jess, you're going to be fine. Do more of that deep breathing." Jamar laughed. "Here, hand me your book bag. If your temper matches your hair, Cooper's in trouble."

Jessie grinned in spite of herself. More relaxed now, they walked down the hall. Jessie noticed the kids who waved or spoke to Jamar. In only a couple of months he had gotten on the student council, the debate team, won great parts in both of the readers' theater productions,

and in the Harriet Tubman play for the Winter Festival—
and he earned excellent grades.

"I'll feel better when this afternoon's meeting is over.
Jamar, how should I act? I worked through some possible
scenarios with my grandmother, but what do you think?"
Jessie looked at him.

They climbed the stairs to the second floor.

"Jess, what do you want? When you leave that room,
how do *you* want to feel?"

"I never thought about it that way," Jessie admitted.

Jamar smiled at some kids and turned his attention
back to her. "You remember when we did that acting ex-
ercise, 'the Machine'? I saw you sitting in the back trying
to figure out where you wanted to be in the machine.
Then you ran up, stood in front of me, and started pump-
ing your arms and legs. You made all of us come alive,
Jessie. Think that way about this meeting."

Jessie's eyebrows shot up. "You remember that? OK.
Still, I don't want to lose my temper or—"

"No, Jess, what *do* you want, not what *don't* you want?"

They were standing by her humanities classroom. Inside she could see Mr. Reynolds writing on a transparency
on the overhead projector.

"I'll have to think about that. Thanks, Jamar."

"We're friends, right?"

"Right," replied Jessie, her cheeks flushed.

Jamar handed over her book bag and started to walk
away. But then he turned back to look at her—and smiled.

Jamar had the kindest, most wonderful eyes in the entire solar system! Mute, Jessie ducked her head and lunged through the classroom door.

Gratefully, she took the seat next to Maria. Just as Mr. Reynolds shut the door, Cooper jerked it open from the other side and eased in. Late as usual.

Jessie directed her attention to the transparency. She had completed the reading for class and a first draft of the essay due on Friday. "Dad would love to see an A in this class," she thought. "I would have gotten one at midterm if I hadn't missed a couple of assignments. But that was before. Like Mamatoo says, 'this is now.' "

At lunch, Jessie headed for the computers in the library. She'd managed to finish her math homework during humanities class. If she spent lunch working, she could get ahead on Greek Mythology, the new unit for humanities. Just for being able to pronounce those ancient Greek names, she deserved a good grade!

Her watch beeped. The forty-minute lunch break had passed too quickly. It was time to get to math, physical education and health, then to Spanish class. Normally, after Spanish would be her new class, History of Drama, and then back to Home Base to finish off the daily marathon. After that there would be rehearsal for Harriet Tubman. Then, toss in a trip to Evergreen Residential Home to entertain the old folks. What a life! But, of course, today was different.

The rest of the afternoon limped along. Jessie kept

glancing at her watch. At 3:00, she had to be outside. Mr. Reynolds knew she'd miss her last classes and the rehearsal. And the Fours knew she couldn't visit Evergreen. Jamar's questions tugged at Jessie. At the end of Spanish class, she handed in her language tape and essay to Mr. Morales and hurried to her locker.

The other Fours—even Cooper—were hanging around in the hall. Julie and Maria lingered by their lockers. Cooper talked to a boy with dreadlocks. Jessie knew why they were all there. They knew about her meeting with Mrs. Grant.

Suddenly, there was a burning hole in Jessie's stomach. Her head hurt. Fumbling with the lock, she leaned her head against her locker. Tears spilled down her cheeks. It was all too much!

"Jess, it's going to be OK," Jessie heard Maria say.

"Don't cry, Jessie," consoled Julie.

Jessie sputtered. "I don't want to go. What if . . . what if . . . ."

Cooper left the dreadlocked boy and joined the other Fours. "Come on, Jessie, you can't let some stupid teacher who's got no business near kids scare you. If you can tell me off, you shouldn't have any problem with her."

Then Jessie felt a hand on her shoulder. She knew that hand belonged to Jamar Lewis.

Wiping her eyes, Jessie turned around.

Maria grinned and handed Jessie a tissue. "Blow your nose, Jessie. Remember, you're a Four."

"We've been through a lot worse," said Julie. "Call me later if you feel like it."

Cooper gave Jessie a closed-fist sign.

"Thanks." Jessie slipped on her jacket.

"Let's go, Jessie Williams. You've got a meeting to make," said Jamar.

Together, Jessie and Jamar threaded their way through the halls to the front door. It was drizzling outside. Jamar waited with Jessie until the familiar beige Volvo station wagon pulled up. Mom waved.

"Everyone gets frightened," said Jamar. "But you can't let fear stop you. Just be yourself, Jessie. That's all you have to do."

Jessie's eyes glistened. "Thanks, Jamar." She ran out to the car.

"Hi, Mom."

"There's a paper bag in the back seat. I know you didn't eat a thing today. So drink that carton of milk and eat the bagel. Your Dad is picking up Mother, and Joe's dropping Cass off. You just relax, honey." Mrs. Williams smiled. "Who was that young man? No, don't tell me. That's Jamar Lewis, isn't it? A very nice first beau."

"He's not my beau, Mom!" Jessie chewed on the bagel. "Jamar and I are friends. Special friends. And that's more than enough for me."

Jessie looked at her mother, the only family member she resembled. Mrs. Williams wore her thick hair in a chignon. Her high cheekbones, full lips, nose, and chocolate-colored skin plus her attractive figure were striking. Mom was the kind of woman that people discreetly stared at. But Mom's real beauty came from inside—from an appreciation of her own beauty and self-worth.

Too soon they arrived at Glenn Elementary School. Closing her eyes, Jessie replayed the various scenes she had practiced with Mamatoo. She reached for her book bag. There was something in there she needed.

Every detail around Jessie stood out vividly. She noticed the way her mother walked with her head high like a queen. The way the rain was falling made her mom's pearl drop earrings seem like two shimmering raindrops on dark velvet.

"Jamar said I have to be myself," thought Jessie. "If I was like Mom, I'd know what to do. I wish I knew who I was, not just on the outside, but on the inside, like Mom." Jessie sighed.

Mrs. Williams glanced back and stretched her hand out. Jessie grabbed it. Only a few kids were in the halls. The school looked older than she remembered, and gloomy. The office was at the end of the hall. The rest of her family stood by the office door. The brass plate in the center of the door was engraved with one word: Principal.

Jessie didn't recognize the man who came out of the door. He was younger than Mr. O'Hara, the principal she had known, and nervous. Where was Mrs. Grant?

"Well, good afternoon, everyone. I'm Mr. Meyers, the principal. It certainly appears that the entire family is here. How . . . how nice." He cleared his throat and shook Mr. Williams's hand. "So good to see you, Mr. Williams, and of course, Mrs. Williams. What lovely daughters you have. You must be Jessie." He reached out his hand and Jessie shook it politely.

"Thank you, Mr. Meyers. Is Mrs. Grant here?" asked Jessie's father, his tone clipped.

"Of course. Now, I think, and I'm sure you'll agree, that having everyone in my small office would make for unnecessary discomfort. I'd like to suggest that only Jessie and I meet with Mrs. Grant," said Mr. Meyers, his eyes darting from one family member to another.

Dad pursed his lips. "My daughter will not go into your office to see that woman without her family by her side. Perhaps you don't realize how serious this situation is for my whole family."

Mr. Meyers put his hands up, his face growing redder by the second. "There should be some way we can compromise."

Jessie was surprised to hear herself speak up. "Dad, I'm not afraid of going in there. But, Mr. Meyers, I have the right to say who I want with me. I want my family. I don't care how crowded it is."

Cass grinned. So did Mamatoo.

"Our daughter has decided, Mr. Meyers," stated Mrs. Williams.

"Now, I hope that we can remember that this is an unusual conference. Staying calm and professional will accomplish what all of us want," the principal stammered.

Jessie watched her father swell up like a bull. That was a dangerous sign. "I suggest that *you* stay calm, Mr. Meyers. And don't make the mistake again of telling me or my family how to act."

"Please, Mr. Williams. I never meant to imply that—"

Jessie interrupted, "Would you open the door?"

Sighing, Mr. Meyers reluctantly entered his office. Jessie followed him. The office wasn't small. There was plenty of room. Just like Mamatoo had played her, Mrs. Grant sat in a chair closest to the principal's chair, partially hidden by the corner of his desk, her hands clenched in her lap. Instead of meeting Jessie's gaze, she glanced from face to face as if she were trying to read a menu.

Jessie took a chair diagonally across from Mrs. Grant. Cass sat on one side of her and Mrs. Williams on the other. Mamatoo and Mr. Williams sat down on the principal's couch, close to Mrs. Grant.

Inside, Jessie chuckled. "My family is too much!" But she stopped when she looked again at Mrs. Grant and the burning in her stomach returned. There wasn't anything funny about what was about to happen.

Mrs. Grant's pale blue eyes were icy. She didn't appear to be concerned or sorry or ashamed. In fact, Jessie's former fourth-grade teacher looked mad, mad to the bone. Shocked, Jessie clutched the arms of the chair. Mrs. Grant was angry! What did *she* have to be angry about?

When Cass took her hand, Jessie realized how cold she

felt. Goose bumps sprang up on her arms. For a moment, she panicked. But the warmth of Cass's hand steadied her. The tension in the office soared.

"Mrs. Grant, do you remember me?" Cass asked.

"Of course I do. How are you, Cassandra?" Mrs. Grant managed a slight smile.

"Not good at all. I'll never forgive you for hurting my sister." Cass nailed each word in the air in front of the teacher's face. "Jess is pretty and smart and talented."

"Now, now. Let's stay with our agenda," said Mr. Meyers. "I believe that Mrs. Grant has something to say. Mrs. Grant?"

Six pairs of eyes swiveled toward her. Mrs. Grant adjusted her glasses with one hand. Then she clasped her hands back in her lap.

"I understand that we are here because Jessie believes that at some time she heard me say something that upset her. Now I have no memory of this. In fact, I can't imagine thinking, much less saying, anything that would hurt a child. However, if Jessie needs an apology, I would never deny her one." Mrs. Grant paused and shifted her weight in the chair. She had been addressing Mr. Meyers the entire time.

Jessie leaned forward and stared at her.

"No, Mrs. Grant, you can't sit there and act like I'm not here! I am here. I want you to look me in the face and apologize to me. That's plain common courtesy." Quickly she checked her grandmother's face. Mamatoo winked. Cass shook her head back and forth in disbelief.

Mr. Meyers cleared his throat. "Jessie, I'm sure that Mrs. Grant didn't mean—"

"Mr. Meyers, our daughter is running this show. Not you," warned Mr. Williams.

Mrs. Grant's eyes bulged. She stared at Jessie. Jessie suddenly recalled dozens of times she had seen that same expression directed toward her before. "Why didn't I realize how much she disliked me?" Jessie marveled. "Because I couldn't. I needed to believe that she liked me as much as she liked Cass."

"Jessie, as I said, if an apology will help you, then you have mine." Mrs. Grant started to rise.

But Jessie got to her feet first. Things couldn't end like this. It wasn't right! "Mrs. Grant, I heard you tell Miss Scott that I was dark-skinned and funny-looking compared to Cass. I heard you say that I wasn't as smart as Cass, that you didn't expect much of me, and that I was a letdown after Cass. You said those mean things about me. I don't need your kind of apology. I don't need you to like me anymore." Jessie looked at her family. "I'm ready to go home."

The family stood up. Jessie reached for her book bag. Briskly, she unzipped the back flap.

"One more thing, Mrs. Grant. I saved my allowance to buy you a birthday card. You gave me this thank you note. Here." Jessie forced the note into the bewildered teacher's hands.

Mrs. Grant's face creased like crumpled paper. "But

I still have that beautiful card you gave me. Jessie, please . . ."

The family stared. The thank you note drifted from Mrs. Grant's hands to the floor. Jessie bent down, picked it up, and laid it on the corner of Mr. Meyers's desk. There was disbelief and confusion in Mrs. Grant's eyes, but Jessie was done.

"Dad and Mom, I'm ready to go home, now," she repeated.

Mr. Meyers stood up. "This meeting certainly went well. I appreciate everyone's cooperation and I'm confident that this matter is fully resolved in a positive way for everyone."

Led by Jessie, the family silently walked out. Mr. Williams shut the door firmly behind them. Hot, heavy tears filled Jessie's eyes, but she batted them back until she was clear of the school building.

In the pouring rain, it was impossible to tell the difference between the raindrops and her tears. Cass hugged her.

"You did great, Jess. I'm so proud to be your sister," Cass murmured, kissing her forehead. "Come on."

Jessie let her sister lead her to the car, away from the school, the office, Mr. Meyers, and Mrs. Grant. The aches and pains were gone, but Jessie felt something else.

She had stood up for herself. "Like when you stand up to a bully, after he's slugged you, chipped your front tooth, and knocked you down," Jessie thought. "Just like that."

The car smelled like wet clothes. Cass comforted Jessie in the back seat, while Mamatoo rode up front with Mrs. Williams. Mr. Williams was on his way back to the bookstore. Eventually Jessie stopped crying and blew her nose.

"Thanks, Cass. I feel so tired, Mom."

"We all do, honey. Do you realize what you did?" Mom braked for a red light and squinted at Jessie in the rear-view mirror.

Cass leaned forward. "I could never speak up the way you did. I can't believe Mrs. Grant tried to ignore you, talking as if you were on another planet, and then having the nerve to say she'd apologize because you felt it would help you!" Cass ranted on, "I think they should fire her from teaching!"

Mamatoo clucked. "Calm down, Cassandra. Mrs. Grant has to live with what she said and did to our Jessie the rest of her life. No matter how hard she tries to deny it. She knows that our entire family was a witness."

"Mamatoo, I'm glad we prepared the way we did," Jessie murmured. "That was a big help. But most of all, it helped having my family there with me."

"I must confess, Jess, I know that I played Mrs. Grant as hard, unashamed, and unrepentant," said Mamatoo. "But I never expected that she would behave with utter disregard for your feelings. You brought honor to our family this afternoon, Jessie Williams. True honor. Isn't that a fact, daughter?"

Mrs. Williams hit the steering wheel with her hands. "Mother, I'm furious! I've prayed Jessie wouldn't go through what I did—being the darkest child in a light-skinned family. She's only twelve. And my baby was barely ten when she heard Mrs. Grant say those awful words."

Jessie reached out. "Mom, don't get upset. I'm going to be fine. I made her look at me. I made her hear me."

Mamatoo leaned back. "Daughter, you know that Jess has to do what we all have to do: learn how to handle people like that. There will be plenty of Mrs. Grants down the line in all colors, ages, and sizes. Now, stop at my favorite deli, then the frozen yogurt shop, and head for home."

Shocked, Jessie's mother protested, "Deli! Frozen yogurt! Mother, this is a serious matter."

"Daughter, serious matters make me seriously hungry. I am in dire need of a smoked turkey sandwich with jack cheese, mayo and lettuce on a sourdough roll with dill pickles, potato chips, and a big mug of peppermint tea. Then a bowl of frozen yogurt—vanilla bean, chocolate eclair, and espresso—with nonfat caramel sauce on top." Mamatoo grinned from ear to ear. "Then, I swear, I'll get very serious."

"Mother!"

Jessie heard her stomach growl. She was hungry, too. Cass's stomach was making noises, too.

"We're hungry back here, too, Mom!" announced Jessie, nudging her sister.

By the time they got home, it was dark. They dropped their wet coats. By silent agreement, they changed their clothes, put on warm robes and slippers, and met back in Mamatoo's living room.

Cass arranged the food on a lacquered tray. Jessie put the frozen yogurt in her grandmother's freezer. Mrs. Williams started a fire in the fireplace. Outside, the rain had stopped, leaving the night sky so sparkling clean that the evening stars glittered like diamond chips.

Muted jazz music played in the background. Sandwiches, napkins, paper plates, pickles, and potato chips were on the coffee table. Jessie snuggled under a woolen throw next to her mother. The teakettle whistled.

Jessie sipped her can of orange soda. The quiet felt like the hush in church just before the first words of the opening prayer are spoken. The exhaustion Jessie saw on the faces around her startled her. They had been as worried and upset about the meeting with Mrs. Grant as she had been. Perhaps more so.

They ate, chatted a little, laughed some, and argued about who got the biggest scoops of frozen yogurt. Mom and Cass cleaned up. Jessie headed upstairs to bed.

Her feeling of relief was short-lived. She had been so consumed with Mrs. Grant that she'd shoved everything else to the back burner. But now there were other problems to deal with—really, one huge problem—raising her grades so that Dad wouldn't make her leave OPA. That wouldn't be easy. Especially with the extra project Mr. Reynolds had assigned.

"Shoot!" she thought. "Blowing my top with Miss Addie Mae "Chuki" Cooper just added more pressure. What in the world can we do together? Mr. Reynolds means business. But so does Dad. He'd ship me to Milton Middle School in a second. Like Mamatoo says, 'I'm out of the frying pan and smack dab in the fire.' I'd better get up and do my homework."

But Jessie couldn't force herself to get up. Instead she pulled the bedspread up to her chin, turned on her side, and fell asleep. Some hours later, she heard the bedroom door open. From the other side of the room came her sister's evenly spaced snores.

It was Dad. He sat down on her bed, took off his glasses, and rubbed his eyes.

"Hi, Dad." Jessie sat up.

"How are you doing?"

Jessie yawned. "Pretty good. I need to get up and do my homework."

He smiled. "You handled yourself well today. I kept wondering, 'Is this my unpredictable, melodramatic daughter acting so mature and brave?' "

"Dad, I couldn't let Mrs. Grant get away with making me feel like nothing."

Her father smoothed her hair back. "I can't think of many kids your age who would have the courage and the poise to speak up the way you did. I am very proud of you, Jessie."

"Thanks, Dad. I'd better get my homework done." She threw the covers back.

But her father didn't move. Instead he embraced her. Jessie stiffened. The last time Dad had hugged her was a year ago right after the fire.

"Jessie, tell me, how do you feel?"

"Fine, Dad, really."

He gazed off. "I don't. A father is supposed to protect his children from anything or anyone who can hurt them. I failed."

"No, you didn't, Dad. I kept what Mrs. Grant did a secret. As soon as you found out, you went to the school. You made her meet with me. And you had faith in me and let me handle the meeting today," Jessie whispered, holding his hand. "Go to bed, Dad. You look tired."

Cass snored on. She slept like a stone. Jessie and Mr. Williams tiptoed out of the room.

"I am glad to see you taking your academic studies seriously. Don't stay up too late." He kissed her forehead.

Jessie gave him the thumbs-up sign, but inside her heart plummeted. Dad didn't understand her at all. And he demanded so much. Too much. Not only did he expect good grades, he hadn't budged about her acting. It remained at the bottom of his list and at the top of hers.

The next morning, the whole family overslept. The rush to get to school and work allowed little time for talk. At OPA, the halls were empty. Jessie hurried to her locker and headed for Home Base.

Jessie got to Home Base right before Cooper. Excitedly, she told Maria, Julie, and a withdrawn Cooper about the meeting. From Cooper she got a quick nod. Maria and Julie quietly cheered.

After taking roll, Mr. Reynolds gave the groups fifteen minutes to discuss their community projects. Presentations were due in three weeks. The Fours pulled their chairs into a circle.

Maria started. "We have to make some decisions. We promised to perform every two weeks for the seniors at Evergreen. I have plenty of pieces to play. So does Julie. We can perform some joint piano and violin pieces."

"So, what's the big deal? Two of us or one of us can

go. Perform for half an hour and leave." Cooper tapped a pencil, "Dancing in front of lonely old people for fifteen minutes is easy."

"I don't know," said Julie. "That's not a real community project. They don't seem unhappy to me. I wonder if they're indulging us. My friend, Mrs. Lee, has a great life, with friends, family, and her painting."

Cooper snorted. "She paints? I thought you were going to say she knits or bakes cookies."

"Cooper, I mean, Chuki, how well do you know that old man you talk to? In fact, other than Julie, how well do any of us know them?" asked Jessie.

Maria doodled while she spoke. "I go to Evergreen. Play some classical music on their piano. Bow when they applaud. Leave. What kind of class presentation will that make? I wouldn't give us a grade above C for doing that. In fact, if C is average, our group is below average."

Jessie's mouth formed a big O. "Don't say that, Maria. You and I have to get a good grade out of this class. We just have to turn this into something more."

Cooper protested. "I am not dedicating myself to a bunch of old folks. I am determined to be selected as a solo dancer in the troupe. Dance is all I have."

Her voice trembled. Jessie noticed her hands shaking, too. Cooper's eyes glistened. She got up and went over to the teacher. The Fours listened.

"Mr. Reynolds, what do we have to do to at least get

a B on this community project?" she asked, her hand on her hip.

"Wrong question, Miss Cooper. Please sit down." Dismayed, the Fours watched Mr. Reynolds eye their group.

Maria leaned forward. "What's wrong, Cooper, I mean, Chuki? What did your father do this time?"

"It's no big deal," said Cooper. When none of the Fours responded, she went on. "OK, Dad called and canceled out again for the weekend. His new baby boy has a cold and his new young wife needs him. I'm used to this," she said, turning away.

"Darn it, Cooper. You just got us into trouble with Mr. Reynolds. If you mess up my grade . . ." sputtered Jessie.

"You'll what? Go crying to your daddy?" Cooper spat back.

"Stop this," ordered Julie. "I just thought of something. Did you see that show on television last week about old people in Japan who are taken care of by the Japanese government?"

Jessie thought. "The one called *Living Treasures of Japan*? That's what they call these old craftspeople, artists, and musicians—living treasures."

With a smile, Julie answered. "Right. Right. They teach their craft, their art, to others so it will live on after they die. It was wonderful. Remember the old man who made those gigantic bells for temples? And the woman who made paper?"

Cooper sighed. "Exactly what is the point?"

Maria waved her arms. "I get it! I get it! We need to interview the folks at Evergreen and see if we have any living treasures there!"

Cooper threw up her hands. "So what if we find three or four of these treasures? Are we supposed to fly them to Japan?"

The other girls ignored her.

"That's great, Julie. We'll see if there are any hidden living treasures at Evergreen," agreed Jessie.

Maria rubbed her hands together. "Sounds like a plan to me. We'll keep a record of the interviews. There could be buried gold at Evergreen. I'm going to check with Mr. Reynolds and see what he thinks. We can go over there today after rehearsals."

Cooper's strident voice interrupted. "This sounds like more work to me. I told you I have to make it into the first line of the African Dance Troupe this year. Nothing is going to stop me."

The three other Fours glared at her. She looked like a living militant history of South Africa in her "Free Nelson Mandela" sweatshirt, South African political buttons, jeans, black boots, and African-American jewelry.

Jessie, Maria, and Julie sighed. As hard as it was, Jessie willed herself to keep quiet. It was Julie who replied.

"Chuki, we're a team. Just go with us today. See what happens." Her voice was gentle, but firm. "OK?"

"Just today, Julie."

It took only a short conversation with Mr. Reynolds to win his approval for their revised project. When class ended, Jessie walked around Cooper to get out.

"Jessie, Chuki, see me before you leave," said Mr. Reynolds.

The room emptied, except for the three of them.

"This is not a conversation," began Mr. Reynolds. "I want to emphasize your joint responsibility for your special project. I don't expect you two to become friends, but I do expect you to come out of the project respecting one another. Or else."

Jessie's stomach flopped. "Or else what?"

"I've decided that this project is thirty percent of your class grade," he replied. "The journal writing starts today with entries every week. The first entry is due next Wednesday. I want a typewritten plan at that time, too. Now make it a good day."

Once outside, the girls separated without speaking. During the day, they avoided one another. Jessie saw Jamar as she was heading for drama class.

"I knew you'd do fine," he said, referring to Jessie's meeting with Mrs. Grant.

"Jamar, it was weird. When she started talking like I wasn't there, I forgot about being scared. Thanks for helping me."

"You did it, Jessie. See you at rehearsal."

Jessie felt a pang because the readers' theater and improvisation class had ended at midterm. That was where she and Jamar had met. Now she would be taking a drama history class—without him.

After their various rehearsals, the Fours went to Evergreen. Cooper lagged behind.

There were nine seniors in the dayroom. Julie went over to her friend Mrs. Lee, an elderly black woman who had lived in the Oakland hills before the fire. Mrs. Lee was afraid to go back there and preferred Evergreen. Jessie watched Mrs. Lee hug Julie. It was Mrs. Lee who had provided the information they needed to find Julie's cat, Toby, who had been missing after the fire.

Maria had befriended two ladies. The three of them chatted and laughed together. Even Cooper had someone. Jessie sized him up, wondering what there was about him that made Cooper hang on his every word. He was a short, stocky black man.

"It must be rough for Cooper, having a father she can't count on," Jessie pondered. "I can't imagine Mom and Dad divorcing and me being the only child. Or Dad marrying some woman half Mom's age and devoting himself to her and their new baby. Dad would never treat me like that." An image of her dad at the meeting with Mrs. Grant came to mind. In spite of everything, she was sure that he would never abandon his family.

Jessie strolled around, smiling at the people sitting here and there. She felt too tired to interview anyone. But she had to. Over in a corner, next to a potted plant, she saw an elegant woman sitting alone, gazing out a window. Jessie recognized her. She always came when they performed. She came in alone and left alone. A dramatic wide streak of silver hair framed the left side of her face. With skin the color of aged pine wood, the lady was like a ripple in a river, disturbing nothing around her.

Cautiously, Jessie approached her. "What is she staring at? The cars in the parking lot?" Jessie wondered.

"Excuse me. I'm one of the girls from the Oakland Performing Arts Middle School."

"I know who you are, Jessie." The sound of her voice startled Jessie. It was deep, like a distant foghorn.

"We're interviewing people to learn about them, like what kinds of special things they used to do or enjoy now," Jessie rattled on, aware that the calm, steady hazel eyes hadn't even blinked. "I don't even know your name." She swallowed, trying to slow down.

"Laura Harding."

On the collar of the white sweater the woman was wearing, Jessie spied a gold locket pin. It was the size of a half dollar. An intricately designed bow decorated the top. Swirls of gold ribbon spilled down the sides of the locket. In the center Jessie made out two initials. Neither matched the lady's name.

"Could I sit with you for a few minutes, Mrs. Harding? If you don't want to be interviewed, we can just look out the window."

"All right."

Jessie waited for her to speak, but the woman remained silent.

"Have you been at Evergreen long, Mrs. Harding?"

"Seven years in April."

Taking a deep breath, Jessie pressed on. "What did you used to do? Were you a teacher or something like that?"

Laura Harding shook her head from side to side. "I never thought of becoming a teacher. My mother certainly wanted me to. But I had a dream to follow."

Jessie was intrigued by this curious answer and quickly tried to think of some way to get this woman to open up.

"Mrs. Harding—"

"Miss Harding, please," corrected the lady.

"I'm sorry." Jessie floundered. "Look, Miss Harding, we're trying to learn more about the people here at Evergreen because maybe some of them have done some great things."

Miss Harding gave Jessie a brief, piercing glance.

Jessie pushed on. "They could be living treasures. We decided that our acting, dancing, and playing a couple of times a month was too one-sided."

Miss Harding sat still, like a portrait. Then she touched the gold locket pin.

"So you want to know if I did great things?" she asked patiently, each word a clear tone.

Jessie bit her lip. "I want to know more about you. Like how you—"

"How I ended up here at Evergreen?"

Miss Harding checked her watch. "Jessie, did it ever occur to you that all people are living treasures? I admit that some may be hidden treasures. I have to leave now."

Jessie got up. "Thank you. I hope we can talk again. Your locket is beautiful."

With a nod, Miss Harding left.

When the half hour was up, the Fours held a conference in the front hall and compared notes. The "Living Treasures" project looked promising. Julie's friend, Mrs. Lee, was an accomplished oil painter who had shown her work in New York City. Mrs. Lee was going to show Julie a portfolio of her best pieces the next time they came.

The smile on Maria's face was as wide as the building. "I can't wait to come back next week and tape-record their stories. They're sisters. Bertha and Beulah Morgan. Never got married. What a life they've lived! Traveled all over the world. Taught school. Bertha was a minister once. Beulah was a show girl! Can you imagine that? I mean, you look at them and all you see are two little old ladies!"

"What about you, Chuki?" asked Julie.

Cooper slapped the side of her head. "Here I've been talking to Mr. Stinson for almost two months and I didn't know the first thing about him. The man is a blues singer. He has composed hundreds of blues songs. He plays the piano and the guitar. And the strangest thing of all—he was playing in Birmingham, Alabama, when the church bombing happened. And he wrote a blues song about it. He calls it 'Birmingham Sunday School Blues.' "

"So, you're glad you came?" asked Julie, daring Cooper to contradict her.

A sheepish grin spread over Cooper's face. "Yeah. Mr. Stinson said he'd play for me next time."

Jessie coughed. "I'm the odd one out. I don't know if Miss Harding is a living treasure or not. I may have to find somebody else. Interviewing her was like talking to a clam."

"Maybe she's shy," suggested Julie. "Why not come back just to visit with her?"

"Maybe." Jessie sounded doubtful.

Maria laughed. "I think we have a real project!"

The Fours agreed.

Heartened, they set off for their respective homes. Jessie had a bus to catch. Outside, she zipped up her jacket. Cooper was walking by herself, heading for the bus to downtown Oakland.

Jessie stopped. Mr. Reynolds had said that the plan for their special project had to be turned in next Wednesday. That left them one week. Reluctantly, Jessie decided to face facts.

"Hey! We have to put something down on paper for Mr. Reynolds," she yelled.

Cooper stopped and hollered back, "I know."

"So?" asked Jessie.

"So what?" Cooper put one hand on her hip.

"Come on, Cooper. We have to do something."

"Your father has this African-American bookstore, right? We can meet there. Call me when you think of something. I'll listen." With that, Cooper took off, leaving Jessie standing alone.

The temperature had dropped. Chilly wind, mixed with fog, blew in Jessie's face. The bus stop was two blocks away. With no one else to talk to, Jessie talked to herself.

"When *I* think of something! Thirty percent of my Home Base grade rides on Cooper. If I get anything lower than a B . . . Between Miss Mouth and Miss Harding, I'm sinking fast." Then Jessie thought about what she'd said to Mrs. Grant—she sure hadn't sunk there. Maybe there was some hope.

Morning light fell on the leaves of the few shrubs around the edges of the house. Cass had already left for cheerleading practice. The rest of the family sat around the kitchen table. Even Mamatoo was up.

"I can't believe it! Tomorrow is—"

"Thanksgiving, Mom," said Jessie, swallowing the last of her grape juice. "We have to get going or I'll be late for school."

Mrs. Williams fretted. "How will I ever get everything done?"

Mr. Williams spoke up. "Relax. You don't have to. We'll help. I'll come home early tonight."

"We have so much to be thankful for this year, Daughter, but one thing and one thing only matters—that we are safe and sound. And, in case you forgot, I know how to cook." Mamatoo's husky voice underscored her words.

"Oh, Mother, I know that!"

"Put on your coat and get going," said Mamatoo, wrapping her robe around her. "Son, don't you dare move. Have a little breakfast with me before you rush to that bookstore."

As Jessie left, she looked back. Mamatoo bustled in the kitchen, chatting away, while a bemused Mr. Williams sat at the kitchen table, just as he had been told to do. "My Mamatoo is too much," she thought.

All the way down the hill, Jessie listened to her mother fuss about Thanksgiving preparations.

"Now, for dinner tomorrow there will be you, Cass, Mother, your father. I hope he remembered to ask Margaret and John. I guess Cass will eat with us and at Joe's house, and he'll do the same." Mrs. Williams slowed down and parked in front of OPA.

Jessie grabbed her school bag. "Thanks, Mom. See you later."

"Jessie, did you invite anyone?"

"No, Mom, not this year."

◇◇◇

When Jessie tried to duck past Mr. Reynolds, his voice reached out and stopped her.

"Good morning, Miss Williams."

"Good morning, Mr. Reynolds," Jessie said softly.

"I expect to see that plan for your special project with Miss Cooper after the Thanksgiving holiday is over," he reminded her with a smile.

Jessie's voice cracked. "I promise not to lose my temper with Cooper again. I have to get good grades or my dad will make me leave OPA. Another project right now is too much."

"She speaks the truth," said Cooper, her earrings tinkling as she moved in behind Jessie. "Mr. Reynolds, we'll get along. I promise. I have so much work, I can't handle more."

Mr. Reynolds regarded them, his face still. "Miss Williams and Miss Cooper, I empathize with you. But I have faith that you two can create a project that teaches you to honestly respect one another. Sorry, shallow promises don't impress me."

Both girls glared at him.

He laughed. "Now, now, now, watch your tempers! That's what got you in trouble in the first place."

During Home Base, Mr. Reynolds made an unexpected announcement.

"For those students enrolled in the History of Drama

course, there will be a change. Mrs. Schubert has had a family emergency. Students in that course will be dispersed to other classes."

Maria and Julie eyed Jessie. "That means you!"

"I know," said Jessie. "I hope I get into a good class. But I'll probably get dispersed to something like scenery design."

Julie teased, "With Jamar?"

Cooper watched.

Jessie blushed. "Stop it! Jamar and I are friends."

Julie smiled, her freckled face relaxed. "Being friends with one of the best-looking and nicest seventh-grade boys at OPA rates pretty high for a lowly sixth-grader."

"What about Jamar being the lucky one?" blurted Cooper.

Maria frowned, "What?"

Cooper threw her hands up. "I'm tired of this . . . this silly, female dribble! What makes Jamar so great? He's a cute boy. So what? Jessie is just as special."

"I didn't mean Jessie wasn't, Chuki," said Julie.

"Julie, think about it," Cooper replied. "Why are girls always the lucky ones? Boys strut around, toss a basketball or football, eat the refrigerator empty, and girls fall all over them. It's disgusting."

Maria snorted, "You sure act happy when you see . . . What's-his-face."

"His name is Kareem, Maria. Kareem Alameen. Kareem and I are equals. As an African-American woman, I respect and celebrate my uniqueness! And so does he, or he's out!" announced Cooper.

The other Fours fell out laughing.

Julie managed to talk. "Well, Chuki Cooper, as a European-American woman, I try my best to celebrate my uniqueness."

"And as a proud Mexican-American bilingual woman, I celebrate my uniqueness whenever I can find the time," Maria said.

Jessie shook her head. "Ditto," she said. "Uniqueness is my middle name! Cooper—Chuki—I should have sent you to face Mrs. Grant in my place!"

Exasperated, Cooper replied, "You don't get it, Jessie. You just don't get it."

Jessie suddenly felt like maybe she didn't get it, after all.

The girls settled down to review their "Living Treasures" project. Everyone except Jessie had plans to visit Evergreen over the holiday weekend. Hearing that, she made a mental note to add one—no, two—more things to her agenda: 1) visit Miss Harding; 2) reflect on her own uniqueness.

As soon as Home Base was over, Jessie dashed off.

"Hey, wait up!" called Cooper.

Jessie halted.

"We have to meet," said Cooper.

"I know," replied Jessie. "I said so yesterday."

"OK. How about meeting around 11:00 A.M., Friday, at your father's bookstore?" suggested Cooper.

"Do you know where it is?" asked Jessie.

"Sure. See you then." Cooper sauntered off. Jessie saw a lanky, handsome boy, his hair in shoulder-length dreads, join her. The two of them could have been members of a guerrilla squad with their combat boots, pants, and jackets.

"Why did I agree to meet her at Dad's bookstore? What can we do together there?" Jessie's mind swirled as she hurried to her next class. Later in the day, she went to her new class. It was in one of the small theaters. Jamar and a group of older student actors stood by the door.

"Jessie, you're in this class? Advanced Improvisation?" asked Jamar.

"Hi, Jamar. Looks like it. You too?"

"Yeah. Come on. Mrs. Shelby goes by the clock," he said, opening the door.

The hour flew by. Improv was a joy for Jessie.

At the end of the formal school day, Jessie headed for the large theater where rehearsals for *Harriet Tubman* were being held. The holiday rehearsal schedule had been posted. No surprise. There would be rehearsals on the Friday after Thanksgiving, Saturday, and Sunday.

Jessie entered the theater and skipped down the stairs. Jamar was seated on stage with the other major actors, including his cousin, Sylvia. They both had big roles, star parts. Sylvia was Harriet Tubman as a young woman and Jamar was her second husband.

Mr. Reynolds was the director. He'd written the play

based on history, with an old Harriet Tubman narrating the outline of her life, and the cast acting it out. There was a chorus, much like the choruses in ancient Greek tragedies.

Thumbing through the marked-up pages of her own script, Jessie reviewed the play in her mind.

The now-famous Christmas raid was the emotional center of Harriet's life, and the play. Acting on a premonition that her brothers were in danger, Harriet Tubman journeyed to the densely wooded forests of Dorchester County, Maryland, at Christmastime. After a series of terrible and frightening adventures, she finally led her brothers—28-year-old Benjamin, 35-year-old Robert, and Henry, age unknown—plus four other slaves across the suspension bridge into Canada. Harriet Tubman later returned and rescued her parents.

◇◇◇

On the bus trip home from rehearsal, Jessie stared out the window. Harriet was on her mind. *There* was uniqueness. There was courage. There was lasting beauty.

Burned-out lots and new partially built houses rushed past. Jessie thought about her father's courageous determination to save their home during the fire, almost at the cost of his life. He had remained behind, keeping the roof wet with garden hoses as the fire sneaked closer and closer.

"Dad's courage," whispered Jessie, seeing her reflection in the window of the bus. The sight of her brown face brought back the memory of Mrs. Grant. The bus ground its way up the hills and around the curves.

"My brown face. My black face. Being an African-American girl does make a difference. To Mrs. Grant, I'd have to be a fair-skinned black girl to be acceptable. To Mrs. Grant, Cass and I are blacks first and human beings second." Jessie sighed. She got up. Her stop was next. "What would I have been to Harriet Tubman? What am I to Dad? What am I to myself?"

The familiar neighborhood sights and sounds of Thanksgiving eve were missing when Jessie got off the bus. She trekked by empty lots with bare foundations. There were only a few houses on the hills.

Traffic was light. Jessie didn't have to glance over her shoulder for cars jammed with kids and holiday groceries. Traffic was always light now. Groups of children playing together outside were ghostly memories. Life would never be the same as before the fire. Jessie searched for her house key and opened the door.

"Child, is that you? Put your books down and come help me."

Jessie stared at the dining room table and then at Mamatoo's satisfied face. She looked like a cat who had caught all the mice.

"Mamatoo, you did all this?" she asked, astonished.

In the dining room, the table was beautifully set with gleaming flowered china, crystal goblets, silverware, and Mom's lace tablecloth and matching napkins. A bouquet of calla lilies, pink roses, and jonquils stood in a vase. She sniffed. Peach cobbler. Mamatoo's buttermilk rolls. Her Louisiana sausage and spicy cornbread dressing.

"Of course! Now, I need you to help me with this turkey," said Mamatoo, her face sweaty. The kitchen was hot.

"Have you been cooking since this morning?" What about getting some rest? Mamatoo, you just had opening night for the play! Didn't the doctor say you should be getting more rest? exclaimed Jessie, worried about her grandmother's age.

The *kente* cloth caftan Mamatoo wore flowed around her feet. Mamatoo kept her hair clipped short. Jessie loved her jewelry—the large cuff bracelets, cowrie necklaces, and earrings. Her grandmother had been going to Africa every year for the past twelve years. She had promised to take Jessie and Cass next year.

With a hoot, Mamatoo placed a large pan of peach cobbler on the tile counter. "Just because I'm old, I have no intention of retiring from life. Rest! How I hate that villainous word! As if one's love of life can only be sparked by passivity. Jessie, my dear, only living life to its fullest can spark the love of life! And you know how I absolutely love rendering your mother speechless!"

Jessie laughed. "Mamatoo, what am I going to do with you? I'll put the turkey in the refrigerator and finish up here. You have a cup of tea and watch me."

An hour and a half later, the two sat quietly at the

kitchen table. The kitchen counter was packed with covered dishes ready to be cooked Thanksgiving morning. Jessie had vacuumed the living room and dusted. The teapot on the table caught the last of the sunlight. Jessie let out a breath.

"So, what is making your heart hurt, child?" asked Mamatoo.

"Mamatoo, when did you find out that being African-American made you different?" asked Jessie, her eyes fixed on the teapot.

"When some silly woman said to me, 'For a little black girl, you're kind of pretty.' I was seven years old and dressed up in my Easter Sunday best. I had on a pink dress with ruffles and tiny green embroidered flowers and new black patent leather shoes." Mamatoo took a sip of tea.

The silence between them stretched. Jessie waited.

"I told that woman that I was pretty anyway and that she was ugly, ugly, ugly. Oh, that woman's face turned red as paint. My mama looked so mad and so sad." Mamatoo's voice halted. "In that moment I knew that being an African-American meant that I was less to many white people." Her voice had dwindled to a whisper.

"Mamatoo, I'm sorry. I didn't mean to upset you," said Jessie, reaching for her hand.

"Child, I'm not upset about me. I'm in a dither about you! It will take me some time to get over what that Grant woman did to you. As black parents, we pray that our children will never have to deal with the prejudice and bigotry that we did. We try to spare them, but we always lose." Mamatoo took a deep breath. "I hate racism!"

Just then the front door opened. Jessie patted her grandmother's hand as she got up to help her mother with the groceries.

"I'll take those, Mom," she said.

"Thanks, honey. I just can't believe how much I have to do. What a day!" Mrs. Williams hung her coat up and turned around.

Jessie watched her mother's mouth open and close wordlessly. Her hand flew up in the air. She started shaking her head and jumping up and down. Mamatoo was laughing her head off.

"*Mother!* What have you done? You did this? How could you? Are you all right? Did you plan this? Jessie, can you believe this?" Mrs. Williams danced into the kitchen. "Did you do this, Mother?"

Choking back laughter, Mamatoo wagged her finger at Jessie's mother. "Daughter, join us for tea."

"Jessie, did you know about this?"

"No, Mom, I was just as shocked as you are. The turkey is in the fridge. The stuffing and the macaroni and cheese are ready. And the dough for the rolls and the cobbler. We can do the vegetables, turkey, and the rest tomorrow morning," she replied.

"Oh, Mother, what a wonderful gift. Thank you." Mrs. Williams kissed Mamatoo's cheek. "Thank you! Thank you!"

Mamatoo waved a slightly trembling hand. "Daughter, don't get your feathers in a flurry. This is simply my way of saying how thankful I am to be a member of this fine family. And to live here with you." She smiled. "I am blessed to be here and not in some home, alone."

"Mother!" cried Mrs. Williams. "You and Dad sacrificed so much to give me a good life. *I'm* the grateful one. Wherever we live, you live. We're family, Mother."

Watching the two women embrace brought tears to Jessie's eyes. She remembered Miss Harding, the solitary woman at Evergreen Residential Home. Jessie wondered if Miss Harding would be spending her Thanksgiving Day at the home, or if she had relatives. Thanksgiving was a bad time to be alone.

"Maybe I should have invited her to dinner. No, that's crazy. She hardly talks to me," Jessie reasoned.

◇◇◇

On Thanksgiving morning, Jessie and Cass prepared the vegetables, cutting squash, green beans, and peppers. Mr. Williams had started the turkey early in the morning. Jessie's mom cooked cranberries and mashed them, mixing in orange peel and juice. Mamatoo was sleeping late.

By 2:00 P.M. everyone was seated at the dining room table. Candles burned at each end. The aroma from the flowers competed deliciously with the food smells. Jessie gazed around the table at their guests. Margaret, a retired school teacher, had worked in the family bookstore for years. She was small and plump, and her eyes revealed a wise intelligence. John had been her father's friend since boyhood. When John retired from the army and was widowed soon after, Dad had persuaded him to work in the bookstore. John always looked a bit confused, but Jessie knew that little escaped his attention. Joe was grinning. This was his first of two Thanksgiving dinners. His own family ate later in the afternoon.

Mr. Williams stood up. "This is a day of thanks. Let us bow our heads. Dear Father, thank you for this gift of family and friends. We are grateful for all that you have given us—the joys and the trials. Our life is stronger. As African-Americans, we give thanks to our ancestors. To the one hundred million African ancestors who died on the Middle Passage. To the enslaved African ancestors who fought for freedom and life. To every African and African-American ancestor, we give thanks. Help us stay strong. And if we fall, help us to stand. Amen."

Silence dissolved into requests for this dish or that, laughter, and much conversation. A couple of times Jessie caught her father's eye. He smiled at her, but each time he did, she recalled his warnings and OPA flashed through her mind. Jessie chewed and swallowed her turkey. She swore by Harriet Tubman and Mrs. Grant: no matter what, she wouldn't leave OPA.

At the evening's end, Jessie finished loading the last of the pots and pans into the dishwasher. She wiped down the counters and covered the remnants of the cobbler with plastic wrap. Margaret and John had left. Cass was with Joe at his family's house. Mamatoo had gone to her apartment downstairs. Mr. and Mrs. Williams cuddled on the couch in front of the fireplace.

The creamy color of the calla lilies caught Jessie's eye. She felt a peace in the house—one that hadn't been there since last year's fire. It was almost as if the house itself was beginning to heal from the firestorm. Outside the window, she saw flickers of light coming from houses below. The charred brick chimneys and foundations, open to the elements, were shrouded in darkness.

Downstairs in her bedroom, Jessie prepared for bed. Her pile of schoolbooks was stacked higher than Cass's. The list of assignments due on Monday flashed before her eyes: two problem sets, a science paper, a take-home essay exam, and three books to read and write reports on. Plus the meeting with Cooper tomorrow morning. And trying to get to Evergreen to interview Miss Laura Harding. Jessie pulled up a chair, chose the math book, and took out her notebook.

In her heart, Jessie knew that she needed to do more to convince her father that she was serious about her studies. There just weren't enough hours in the day. But Dad required proof. Solid proof.

The sun was bright. Jessie checked her watch. She had to meet Cooper at the bookstore in less than an hour. Cass's bed was empty and impeccably made. As usual. Forty-five minutes and two buses later, she entered the bookstore. Cooper stood inside, near the door.

"So, you made it. I thought you might back out. I love this bookstore," said Cooper, staring around. "You're lucky, Jessie."

"Why?"

Cooper shrugged her shoulders. "Come on, Jessie. Everything in the world you could ever want to know about African-Americans is right here."

"Well, not everything, young lady. But I will take that as a compliment," said Mr. Williams. He held out his hand.

"I'm Chuki Cooper. This is an honor. Thanks to you, I can read about David Walker and Martin Delany and even poor, misunderstood Phillis Wheatley," Cooper said, stretching out her own hand.

Jessie stepped back. Her father was actually grinning.

"Now, Chuki, what do you know about Phillis Wheatley being misunderstood?" He shook her hand and stood there with his arms folded, with a big-as-a-barn-door grin on his face.

Cooper grinned back.

Jessie wanted to gag! They acted like a mutual admiration society.

"You said my name right! Well, in the spring of 1772, Phillis Wheatley, a young African girl, was forced to take an oral examination given by eighteen prominent white Boston men. One was John Hancock, a signer of the Declaration of Independence. She was tested to see if it was possible for an African to write the poems she claimed were hers. We don't know exactly how they tested her, but they did write a public letter saying she wrote those poems."

Mr. Williams clapped. "Outstanding, Chuki! Few people know that story about her. In that public letter those Bostonians referred to Phillis Wheatley as—"

"An uncultivated barbarian from Africa," finished Cooper, the smile on her face stretching across the street.

"You are remarkable, Chuki! If more people knew about the real trials of that unusual poet, they would be more sympathetic." He patted Cooper on the shoulder. "Outstanding. Your parents must be so proud of you."

"So, is this test over? Dad, Cooper and I need to use the Author Room," Jessie interrupted.

They stared at her, as if she were an interloper.

"In a minute, Jessie," said her father, turning back to Cooper. "This is the first friend of yours who has such an interest in our history. I'm glad that you finally have friends like Chuki."

"Look, Dad, we're not exactly friends. We've got this project to plan. It's kind of an emergency," Jessie said, talking fast. "So we have to get to work."

"Jessie, you could learn a great deal from Chuki. Young lady," he turned back to Cooper. "Do you have any special interests? I may have some books for you to look at."

Impatient, Jessie tapped her foot.

"Famous African-American dancers, Mr. Williams. I plan to become one." Cooper beamed, her *kente* cloth turban wound brightly around her head. "But my studies, especially black history, are important to me."

"Dad, Cooper adores Judith Jamison." Jessie's voice was as dry as the Sahara Desert.

But her father was already walking to a far corner of the bookstore, near the Author Room. Cooper followed him. Feeling like a tagalong, Jessie drifted behind, within earshot.

"Chuki, here are several books about the Alvin Ailey dancers, and a couple on Judith Jamison." He pointed to a row of books. "Feel free to look at them."

Cooper bent down and handled the books as if they were cartons of eggs. She opened each one. When she gazed up, her face was glowing.

"These are wonderful, Mr. Williams. I never knew they existed. I found some material about Judith Jamison in the library, but these are brand-new."

"I thought you knew everything," Jessie said, immediately wishing she could snatch the words and stuff them back in her mouth. The expression on her father's face made her cringe. "I mean, you do know a lot, Cooper."

Mr. Williams glowered at Jessie. "Sometimes my daughter speaks before she thinks. Now, Chuki, enjoy the books," he said. "Be careful with them."

Jessie simmered beneath the beamed ceiling, where a fan slowly revolved. African sculpture, baskets, and swatches of cloth decorated the walls. Easy chairs and wooden benches dotted the room. Customers read quietly in some of them.

In the children's section, dolls and stuffed animals were strewn around the brightly colored rug. A lot of books were read on that rug—by Margaret, parents, and occasionally a real storyteller.

"Follow me," Jessie said to Cooper.

The Author Room was where visiting black authors

came to read their works and autograph books. Mr. Williams enjoyed a reputation as a strong supporter of authors. Many who earned fame returned to the bookstore regularly in appreciation of his support.

Posters of famous authors—Toni Morrison, Zora Neale Hurston, James Baldwin, Ernest Gaines, and others—hung on the walls. The flags of several African nations were draped from the ceiling. A wooden podium stood in one corner. The names of the authors who had read there were carved into it. Behind a door were dozens of folding chairs, stored away until the next reading. Jessie walked over to a round table.

"OK. What are we going to do for this project?" Jessie sat down, opening her notebook, a pen poised in her hand.

Cooper ignored Jessie. She ran her hand over the glossy cover of the book with Judith Jamison pictured on the front.

"Jessie, you don't know how lucky you are, do you? You've got the best father. And this bookstore!" Cooper threw up her hands. "If I had this, I'd always be happy."

"Everything that glitters is not gold," muttered Jessie.

"Maybe you couldn't tell gold from brass if it was right smack in your face, Jessie Williams," snapped Cooper.

Jessie struggled to control her temper. "Look, Cooper, you know it's either a B grade or Milton Middle School for me, so let's get this project together."

Forty minutes later they hadn't made any progress.

Margaret checked in. Seeing their sour faces, she left. When she returned a half hour later, both girls had their heads on the table.

Margaret took a seat at the table. "I'm on break. Your father told me what you two are up to. I haven't taught middle school in some years, but I might be able to help. Explain the assignment to me."

While Cooper explained, Jessie felt more dejected.

Jessie shook her head. "Margaret, Cooper and I will never be able to do this."

"You're right about that," said Cooper, who started pacing.

"Let's maintain an optimistic point of view," chided Margaret. "What could you both do for this project that would require the least interference with your lives?"

"Let me dance while Jessie acts," said Cooper.

Jessie spoke up. "I'll vote for that."

Clapping her hands, Margaret rose up. "So there's your project."

The girls stared at her.

"Why can't you two support one another through your talents?" asked Margaret. "Jessie, you watch Chuki dance. Chuki, you watch Jessie act. See what happens."

Both girls watched Margaret leave.

"So, am I supposed to come to your practices and you come to mine?" asked Cooper.

"That's a place to start. At least we'd have a plan to turn in and something to write in our journals to Mr.

Reynolds," said Jessie. "We're rehearsing tomorrow morning. You could come to that. I'll come to one of yours."

Cooper leaned back in her chair. "Give me another option. I may have something better to do."

Jessie's simmering pot blew its top. "Look, Addie Mae Cooper, I need your cooperation!"

"Don't you call me Addie Mae!"

"You know what? You've got major problems. You need to do some serious thinking," yelled Jessie.

"About what, Miss Know-it-all?"

"About that little girl who was killed in the bombing—your relative. I'd be proud to be named after Addie Mae Collins. Her name would live on with me." Jessie put her hands on her hips.

"Mind your own business! Just give me your rehearsal schedule and I'll give you mine," said Cooper, gathering up the books, "I'm going up front to read."

"I am, too." Jessie surprised herself. The thought of leaving Cooper in the bookstore alone, reading, well . . . "If she's going to stay here and read, so will I."

Later, from the comfort of a cushioned chair, she watched Cooper examine each shelf of books. With customers browsing and buying, it was all Mr. Williams could do to keep up. John and Margaret were on their lunch break. It seemed as if a sudden swell of people had hit the store. Jessie started to get up to help.

Astonished, she watched Cooper go up to customers, ask them what they looking for, and direct them to the appropriate area. Cooper was answering questions! After a brief conversation with Dad, Cooper used the computer to see if a requested book was in stock!

"Who does that girl think she is? Coming in here and taking over! I'll show her! This is my family's store!"

Jessie edged around customers and stalked up to the counter. Before she could open her mouth, her father's smile pinned it shut.

"Jessie, while Chuki helps me up here, I'd like you to set up the Author Room for a reading. Then you need to get home." He handed a man his credit card. "You have homework."

"I'd rather work up here with you," she protested.

"Jessie, please," he warned.

"When I leave, you leave," whispered Jessie to Cooper.

"Sure, no problem." Cooper hit a few keys on the computer and grinned at the couple waiting. "We have that book in stock. Two aisles over, under Autobiography. Here, I'll show you."

Jessie stood fixed, her mouth open. "Where did she get that *we* from?" she yelled inside her head. "She's not employed here. She's not a part of my family!" A gesture from her father told Jessie to get going.

Chairs slammed down, hitting the floor with a metallic thud. Impatient, angry mutters peppered the air. The podium jerked across the floor to the center of the Author Room. Jessie stomped from one end of the room to the other.

"Jessie, what in the world is going on in here?" yelled her father.

"Nothing, Dad."

"You're making enough racket to wake the dead!"

Jessie faced him. "Dad, Cooper's got a lot of nerve! She walks into *our* family bookstore and takes over. You hardly ever let me look up a book on the computer. And you just let her use it, Dad." Tears welled in her eyes.

"Jessie, I don't have time for your theatrics. You exaggerate everything. Your friend was simply kind enough to step in."

"She's not my friend!"

"Well, she should be. You could learn a lot from Chuki, Jessie," Mr. Williams asserted—again—his face stern.

Just then, the room seemed to shrink, closing in on Jessie. She grabbed her jacket and scurried out of the store. Just outside the door, Jessie stared back in through the window.

Beyond the book display, she saw her father shake his head at her and then turn his back—to talk to Cooper. All of the old feelings of not being pretty enough, smart enough, or good enough for her father returned. With tears streaming down her face, Jessie brushed past Margaret and John returning from lunch and ran off.

She kept asking herself the same question over and over again. "Why doesn't Dad love me?"

"**J**essie! Wait!"

Jessie felt someone grab her arm.

Cooper held up her hand as she fought to catch her breath. "I just ran . . . three blocks. Don't . . . you . . . dare . . . move."

Jessie jerked her arm away. "I don't care how far you ran, Cooper. Why don't you run back to the bookstore? You belong there more than I do."

"I was just helping out," Cooper said defensively. "Look, I'll be at your play rehearsal tomorrow morning. You need to come to one of my dance rehearsals next week. Here's the schedule." Cooper thrust a piece of paper into Jessie's hand. "You are so lucky, Jessie Williams. I don't know why you can't see it."

"There's a lot you can't see, Cooper!"

"What? Name one thing, Jess."

They glared at each other.

"Number one: that is my father, not yours. And that goes for the bookstore, too. Number two: your real name. Why do you hide the fact that Addie Mae Collins was related to you? Why can't you keep one name? Her name?" Like flashing siren lights, Jessie's eyes blazed.

But Cooper looked more hurt than angry. She fingered one of her beaded braids.

"I can't deal with you," said Cooper bluntly. "Let's just show up at rehearsals each week and write in those dumb journals. I'll type up our plan for Mr. Reynolds. You're an actress. Act like we're getting along."

The trip home went much faster than the trip to the bookstore. By the time Jessie hopped off the bus, she'd decided to do whatever she could to win her father's approval—short of going to Milton Middle School.

Joe was at the kitchen table, eating. A plate of turkey sandwiches sat in front of him along with a bag of potato chips and a dish of pickles. Cass was filing her nails.

Jessie knew where her mother was: the day after Thanksgiving was a major shopping event. Mamatoo was at the theater. With rave reviews, her repertory company was playing to capacity audiences.

In minutes, Jessie had loaded a plate of her own. She

balanced a can of root beer on the plate and headed downstairs. Friday's rehearsal was for the major parts only, so by evening Jessie had most of her homework done. She pulled the *Harriet Tubman* script out.

As Harriet Tubman's younger sister, she had enough lines to fill a teacup. But as a member of the chorus, she had numerous lines and chants to memorize, and blocking to remember. The chorus would stand down-right on the stage throughout most of the scenes, but their movements were particularly important. Jessie reviewed them repeatedly, feeling the rush of excitement even sitting alone in her room.

Much later, asleep in her bed, Cass snored. Jessie looked at the clock. It was past midnight. She laid the script down.

◇-◇-◇

On Saturday morning, a drowsy Jessie reached school early for rehearsal. She needed to get in some computer time first. Other students were also in the open library, but Jessie found a free computer. She punched the keys to open the database she wanted. In seconds, she was online, scanning newspapers for September 15, 1963, the day a little girl named Addie Mae Collins was killed with three other girls in a church in Birmingham, Alabama. She read about the man glutted with hate who had bombed the church on a Sunday morning when the church basement would be filled with children attending

Sunday school. The man had wanted to kill the children because they were black.

With pen in hand, Jessie noted the important facts. The photographs of the bombing shocked her. She shrank inside when she saw the photographs of the four dead girls. The articles made it clear that the bombing had fueled the Civil Rights Movement of the 1960s and early 1970s. In fact, the girls were murdered only weeks after Dr. Martin Luther King Jr. had given his "I Have a Dream" speech. The death of Cooper's relative had made a whole country wake up. Jessie hit the print button and collected copies of the most comprehensive articles. Then she dashed off to rehearsal.

Behind the scenes, older students were working on costumes, sets, and props. This play had first been produced six years ago, but Mr. Reynolds had taken this opportunity to make a few changes. He was explaining this to the rest of the cast. Jessie glanced around. No Cooper. Good.

For the next two hours, Jessie concentrated on following Mr. Reynolds's directions. Being a member of the chorus was indeed as much of a responsibility as she had thought. Occasionally, out of the corner of her eye, she watched Jamar rehearse. It was clear why he had won the part: Jamar labored to be the best and he took correction well.

Jessie's stomach knotted at the stern tone of Mr. Reynolds's directions. Mr. Reynolds could be tough, but

Jamar nodded and did what he was told. If it didn't work, he and Mr. Reynolds would confer until they came to an understanding.

Finally, rehearsal ended.

"Hey, Red, some of us are going to get food. Come on," said Jamar. "I'll walk you to the bus stop afterward."

Jessie hesitated. Dad didn't want her going with any boy to get anything. "What if I go? Who will know? This isn't a date, not technically," she thought. Then she caught sight of Cooper. Cooper had been perched up in the shadows the whole time! She watched as the strange, wiry girl got up and left.

Jessie smiled at Jamar. "OK. I have to get my jacket and books. And stop calling me 'Red'!" She would have to do something about the color of her hair.

Sitting on a plastic seat at the local fast food place, Jessie felt especially happy to be out with her fellow cast members—her own community—and Jamar. Most of them were seventh-graders, too, which made it all the more special. Just as she was biting into a jumbo bean burrito overflowing with fixings, the door opened and Jessie felt a rush of cold air. She shivered and looked up. She practically jumped out of her skin. It was Dad!

"Oh, no, this can't be happening to me!" Jessie ducked her head and tried to melt into the seat. She peeked. Dad didn't act as if he had seen her.

The door opened again. It was Cass! Catching her sister's eye, Jessie gave her a pleading look. Before their father could turn in Jessie's direction, Cass blocked him, talking fast and pointing up to the menu.

Jessie remembered that the bathroom was behind her. If she could casually get up and walk eight feet without Dad seeing her, she could hide out until he left. Quickly, she pulled her cap over her bright red hair. Easing up, she glided the eight feet, her eyes glued to the floor. In the bathroom, she rushed into a stall and locked the door. Jessie's heart pounded.

Fifteen minutes later she stuck her head out around the bathroom door. Dad and Cass were gone. Jessie joined the others, but she was not hungry anymore. Seeing her father had spoiled her mood.

On the way to the bus stop, Jessie spied a drugstore.

"Jamar, will you wait for me here?" she asked.

She searched the aisles, finally finding what she needed. Jamar ran with her to the bus stop. They could see the bus coming. Jessie leaped aboard and waved good-bye.

By the time her father came home, Jessie was in bed, the script in her hand. It had been a relief to learn from Cass that Dad hadn't spotted her. The bedroom was quiet. Cass was out with Joe.

"If I can learn the chorus' lines for Act I, I'll be ready for rehearsal on Monday." Sunday's rehearsal was a tech rehearsal only. She positioned herself in front of the mirror on the back of the bedroom door and began to read her lines.

But instead of concentrating on her part, Jessie kept seeing herself in the mirror. Mrs. Grant would never realize what she had said or done. And her dad would never understand her.

Jessie shook herself loose from these thoughts and found herself focusing on her hair. The red seemed to be getting redder and redder! It would take months for the brash, loud color to grow out. Being called "Red" by Jamar hadn't helped.

Jessie stood there and reasoned with herself. "What if I cut it just a little? That leaves less red to grow out. Or maybe I should wait until tomorrow and ask Mom. Or I could leave it this length and . . ."

Decision made, she grabbed the hair dye she had purchased at the drugstore. Dad and Mom were upstairs. This was the night they worked on the accounts for the bookstore. They'd be occupied for hours.

Jessie made sure she had her watch. There would be no going to sleep with the color on this time. That was how she'd gotten flaming red hair in the first place. Following the directions, she mixed the color with the solution; snipped the tip of the bottle; and shook it vigorously. Then she put on the plastic gloves and began to apply the jet black hair dye. After twenty minutes, Jessie rinsed out the color, applied the special shampoo and conditioner, and washed her hair.

Confident and proud of herself, Jessie looked in the mirror. What she saw made her scream. Her hair wasn't red anymore. It was one thousand percent pure BLACK! The kind of yucky black she'd seen on wigs. Worse, her hair stuck out in all directions. Hard, brittle, bone-dry hair.

In shock, Jessie looked at her hand. There was hair in her hand. Real hair. Black hair. Her hair. Visions of a bald Jessie Williams gripped her like a nightmare. Jessie searched for her mother's conditioner. She poured it on and massaged it in. Someone knocked at the door.

"Jessie? What are you doing in there?" came her mother's voice.

"Mom, help me!"

Mrs. Williams opened the bathroom door and let out a gasp of dismay.

"Jess! Not your hair! Don't tell me you dyed it again."

"I thought if I bought some different dye . . ."

"Where's the package? What color is it, Jess? Jet Black! Permanent hair color! We'll be lucky if you don't end up losing your hair. Didn't I say just be patient?" Mrs. Williams rinsed out Jessie's hair.

Ten minutes later Jessie sat at the kitchen table, smelling like mayonnaise. Mom had worked half of the jar through her hair and wrapped a warm steamed towel around her head.

"Mom, I smell like a sandwich. Will the smell stay? I can't go to school smelling like mayonnaise," she said. "Am I going to be bald?"

Mrs. Williams checked Jessie's hair under the towel. "I hope not."

"Oh, no," wailed Jessie. "Mom, please, save me!"

"I'm doing my best. We have to wait and see."

Mr. Williams gazed up, his fingers still atop of the keys of the adding machine.

"I do not understand you." He rubbed his eyes. "We never had this hair coloring problem with Cass. Your hair is fine. Why won't you leave it alone?"

Instead of answering, Jessie slumped in her chair. The sound of the adding machine continued: one third of the book sales for the year rode on the weeks from Thanksgiving to the end of Kwanzaa.

Jessie's mother handed her husband a bowl of chili. "Eat, honey. This is just a stage. Every girl goes through adolescence in her own way." Mrs. Williams unwrapped the towel and handed Jessie a newly steamed one. "You were talking about John before I went downstairs to see about Jessie."

Between bites, Mr. Williams spoke. "John has a bad flu. So he'll be out for at least a week. As busy as the store is, it still would be better for him to stay home for a couple of weeks and get his rest."

"That's going to leave you short-handed."

"I know."

"Dad, I could help out at the bookstore. I know how to do everything," said Jessie.

He dismissed her. "You have to concentrate on school. I don't want to have to transfer you to Milton, but if those grades aren't up, I will, Jessie."

"But, Dad . . ." insisted Jessie, thinking of her plan to win her father's approval.

Her father looked at her hair, rolled his eyes, and nothing more was said.

That night, Jessie woke up sniffing. She smelled mayo. Mom had said it was just her imagination. Jessie patted her head. Mom had rinsed out the mayo and washed her hair in some super gentle shampoo, then rolled it on soft rollers.

When Jessie unrolled her hair Sunday morning, the good news was that it wasn't falling out. The bad news was that she still smelled like mayonnaise. Her hair just hung there, like cooked spaghetti. It looked awful. Cass sat Jessie down in a chair and experimented with different styles.

"You have two choices. Pull it back and use my barrettes. Or pull it back and use my barrettes." Cass giggled.

"This isn't funny! I'm a disaster!"

"Almost, but not quite," said Cass, laughing.

❖❖❖

By Monday afternoon, Jessie was pooped. She'd hidden her hair under a black scarf. Classes, assignments, rehearsal, and curious looks from the other kids proved to be too much. Her head pounded. But she had to go to

Evergreen and talk with Miss Harding. The other girls had gotten far more information than she had. She was the only Four who had next to nothing.

Zip. Zero. Zap. If Miss Harding didn't cooperate she would have to select someone else as a potential living treasure.

"I hope Miss Harding talks to me. When I called her this morning she said I could come by. Maybe she has some aspirin," Jessie muttered to herself, dragging along her book bag.

A cold wind blew in her face. Dark clouds bunched up like grapes. Jessie searched the sky for some sign of blue. There was none. Just as well, it fit her mood.

Evergreen Residential Home stood on a corner surrounded by lush landscaping, thanks to Maria's father, who owned a successful landscaping business. The windows reflected the dull sky. Jessie sat in the dayroom waiting. Minutes passed. Restless, she stared around at the few people in the room. Were any of them living treasures? Finally, the door opened. There she was.

"Miss Harding, hello!" said Jessie. "Thank you—I mean, for letting me visit you."

"Jessie, how are you?"

"My head hurts," she answered.

"Stress," said Miss Harding.

"And being an almost-adolescent," said Jessie. "Do you have any aspirin?"

"I don't believe in pills. Follow me."

They went out the dayroom door, past the welcoming area, down two long hallways, and into a huge kitchen. Jessie had never been outside the dayroom. The kitchen was grand. A large butcher block table stood in the center. Shiny copper pots and pans hung above.

A woman came out of the meat locker carrying a large leg of lamb. She nodded at Miss Harding and put the meat down on the butcher block. It was plain to see that she was the cook.

There was a huge refrigerator, an even larger stove, and lots of cabinets. Over the stainless steel sink was a greenhouse window. Ferns, grape ivy, and geraniums made the room light and airy. There was a round table by the sliding glass doors.

"Sit there." Miss Harding pointed to a chair at the table. "This is Mrs. Davis, our cook." They nodded to each other.

Obediently, Jessie sat down and watched as Miss Harding took out tea and set water to boil. She placed mugs on the table with a basket of apples and bananas. Then she placed rice cakes on a plate next to a jar of peanut butter. Jessie saw that it was natural peanut butter like Mamatoo bought. In fact, the whole table could have been a Mamatoo table.

Slowly and gracefully, the silent woman poured tea the color of new grass into Jessie's mug, then her own. She sat down. Jessie sipped the tea and took the rice cake with peanut butter Miss Harding handed her.

Outside, gusts of wind swirled around the garden. Plants and bushes swayed as if to music. Wooden benches framed the grassy borders. A bird feeder dangled from one of the evergreen trees.

Layer by layer, the tension drained from Jessie and with it, her headache. All the demands of her life, including the threat from her father, were held at bay by the peace in the kitchen.

Cautiously, Jessie peeked at Miss Harding. She was dressed in a plain navy dress and sweater, which made the gold locket pin look all the richer. That streak of silver hair lent the elderly woman a special elegance. A small pearl earring dotted each ear.

"Better?"

Jessie smiled. "Much better, Miss Harding. Thanks. What kind of tea is this?"

"A special herbal blend."

"Well, it's sure helping. Can the people who live here come back and use the kitchen anytime they want to? Like in a real home?" asked Jessie.

"Not quite. Regular meals are served here. That's why we have Mrs. Davis."

"Then why can you use it, Miss Harding?" Jessie lifted her mug to her lips.

"I own Evergreen, Jessie. This is my home."

Tea sputtered from Jessie's mouth.

"You do? You? You must be rich!" exclaimed Jessie.

"No, not rich." Miss Harding smiled. "So, are you still going to interview me? As a living treasure?"

It was the first time she had really smiled. Jessie spied warmth in her eyes and a hint of hurt.

"Sure." She wondered where to start. "Why don't you live in a regular house?"

Miss Harding rested her chin on her hand. "I did for a time. But I was always coming down here, so I decided to move in. Many of the people here are my friends."

"Your friends? So they don't have to pay? What a deal!"

Miss Harding chuckled. "They pay what they can afford."

Jessie continued. "Miss Harding, what did you do? I mean, for a living? For work?"

Miss Harding stood up and pushed her chair back in its place. "Jessie, I think that's enough for today. There's a storm coming. You should get home."

"Can we talk again soon? Please?" asked Jessie, putting on her jacket.

Cocking her head to one side, Miss Harding fingered the locket pin.

"Yes, Jessie, we can talk again. Now hurry home."

On the way home, Jessie watched the rain stream down the windows of the bus. For over two months she had been going to Evergreen.

"I thought we were the ones helping out a bunch of

lonely, poor, old people. I thought that they needed us desperately. And all that time we were in left field. Shoot, we were out of the ballpark," Jessie mused. "They're all Miss Harding's friends. I can't believe Miss Harding owns Evergreen."

◇◇◇

On Tuesday, Jessie tugged her scarf tighter around her head and went in search of Cooper's jazz dance class. Cooper had talked to her dance teacher and obtained permission for Jessie to sit in the corner and observe. Cooper wore a tired black leotard with black tights and soft black shoes. There were three lines of five dancers, boys and girls. They were just finishing the warm-up. Jessie leaned against the wall.

An angular woman with short blond hair ran the class. Soon, sweat glistened on the bodies of the dancers as the teacher led them through a series of exercises. The language of dance was so different from the language of acting—leg extensions, front, side, and back; turns, leaps, and hops across the floor. Cooper seemed to belong to this world. All of her attention was directed at her teacher.

"This is eight counts," began the teacher, talking the students through a new movement. "Now, step forward onto your left foot, *battement,* right leg to the front, arms in second position. Step on the right, step behind the right with the left and side again with the right . . ."

The dancers moved to the sounds of bossa nova jazz.

Cooper executed each part of the short combination with deliberate concentration and the teacher nodded her approval. For the next hour, Jessie sat mesmerized. She wished she had the trained, limber body of a dancer.

That night, Jessie opened a small notebook. This would be her first entry. Mr. Reynolds wanted it turned in tomorrow. From a drawer full of pens, she selected a blue pen decorated with rainbows. Mamatoo had given it to her.

> Dear Mr. Reynolds,
>   I went to see Cooper at her jazz dance class. I stayed over an hour. Dancing is hard, sweaty work. I'm glad I'm an actress. That's all.

Jessie closed the book and stuck it in her book bag. After carefully combing her hair and rolling it, she tied a silk scarf around her head. Her reflection in the bathroom mirror stared back at her. "So, Jessie Williams," it seemed to say, "you made up your mind to stay at OPA and study. When are you going to make up your mind about your hair and the rest of you?"

"Jessie Williams, I can't believe it!" Julie was the first one to speak.

"No! No way!" Maria exclaimed.

Only Cooper sat quietly, taking in Jessie's news about Miss Harding.

Mr. Reynolds walked over. "Fours, what is going on here?"

Everyone stared at Jessie. Today she had covered her hair in a pea green scarf.

"I found out that one of the ladies at Evergreen is the owner."

Mr. Reynolds grinned. "Excellent. But I'd still like

your journal and Miss Cooper's, plus the description of your plan. You may pick up your journals at the end of the day. And next week I want to have a conference with both of you."

When Cooper handed her journal and the plan to Mr. Reynolds, her eyes met Jessie's. They were both wondering the same thing. What had they written about one another? Only Mr. Reynolds would know.

In history class, Jessie struggled through a surprise essay examination. When time was called, she still had two questions left to answer.

Next, she was stunned by a pop math quiz. She solved the problems quickly, but half of the points lay in written explanations of how and why she solved them in the way she did. It was torture trying to explain how her mind worked and what made mathematical sense to her.

At one point, Jessie threw her pencil down and almost fled the room in frustration. She didn't think in a one-two-three sequence. Her mind leaped to answers almost immediately. Then it swooped around, putting the parts together. How could she write that down?

When she handed her test in and left, she felt depressed. On an impulse, she snatched Cooper's schedule out of the pocket in her book bag. Scanning it, she hurried down the hallway.

Carefully, she opened the door to the small auditorium and eased into a seat in the back. Drums blasted from speakers on the stage. Members of the African

Dance Troupe milled about. A man, bearded and bald, tapped the floor with a carved stick. Behind him a woman dressed in a black leotard and a multicolored head wrap switched the music off. The girls lined up in three rows. Cooper was in the back.

Sure that she wasn't seen, Jessie watched. The male teacher carried a large skin drum to the front of the stage, off to the right. He sat down on a chair and placed it between his legs. The lines moved to the beat of the drum, following the lead of the female teacher.

Suddenly, five dancers moved to the front as the lines danced back. Cooper wasn't one of the featured dancers. Jessie watched her. Why didn't these teachers see how good Cooper was?

Jessie took out a notebook and started doodling as she sat in the dim light. Her doodles became bits of sketches and then real sketches. Jessie recalled that she hadn't sketched anything since last summer. She had forgotten how soothing drawing was.

When the practice session concluded, Jessie started to leave with everyone else. Only then did she notice that Cooper stayed behind on the stage. Jessie immediately sat down again. Cooper went to her dance bag and took out a cassette player. Jessie scrunched down in her seat. Cooper turned on the music.

Organ music. A choir, singing a gospel sound. An old, melancholy sound, so old and so sad. Cooper walked to the center of the stage. Head lowered, she defined the air around her with her arm movements. Entranced, Jessie didn't blink as Cooper moved through step after step, composing and changing as the music played.

Jessie could imagine her own ancestors laboring under the sun, not as people, but as things, slave things, with no human rights. The sun, sweat, tears, and voices grieving and singing this desolate song. She swayed in time to the beat.

Without warning, Cooper jumped up and down—hard—and began running around the stage frantically. Then she dropped to the floor, head bent, her body shaking.

In that movement, Jessie understood what Cooper was doing. Cooper was using her dance to tell the story she couldn't express in words. She was dancing her most private emotions and thoughts. Hoping she wouldn't be seen, Jessie ducked as low as she could and began to sketch quickly.

When Cooper stood up, her hands wound around her body, fluttering like wings. With long strides, she danced to every corner of the stage. Each time the music shifted, Jessie experienced something new. Gospel music. Civil rights protest songs. The Black National Anthem. Cooper danced as if she were fighting, grieving, and struggling. Then she fell to her knees, head raised, with her hands in prayer. Jessie's eyes watered. Finally, Cooper turned the music off, gathered her belongings, and left the stage. Jessie waited until she was sure she could sneak out safely.

"I can't believe it!" Jessie thought. "Cooper is dancing the story of Addie Mae Collins and the Sunday school bombing! Composing her own dance. And is she good! But I can't tell her I saw her. I can't tell anyone."

At the end of the school day, Jessie waited as Mr. Reynolds wrapped up Home Base. Rattling off a list of events, he ended with the announcement of the holiday dance on December 18th and news that at the very least, a preview of their community service projects would be due before vacation. That meant in two weeks. The Fours eyed one another. They were nowhere near being ready!

"We have to meet, if only for five minutes." Maria tossed back her long black hair. "I'll be late for piano class, but we have to come up with a plan and execute it ASAP."

There were dark circles under Julie's eyes. Her skin was paler than usual; her sprinkles of freckles stood out. She passed her hand across her eyes.

"Toby doing all right?" asked Cooper. "You don't look so good, Julie."

"Toby's fine. It's my folks fighting again. The insurance company won't settle fairly," said Julie, wiping her eyes. "We used to be happy. I wonder if we'll ever have a real home again."

"I know about that," Cooper said, digging in her book bag and handing Julie a tissue. "I learned one thing. Stay out of their mess. Parents do what they want to. Concentrate on your violin, your music."

"Thanks, Chuki." Julie managed a smile, "Sometimes I wish they would divorce. At least the arguing would stop."

"No, you don't. Divorce is the pits, too." Cooper stared at the floor. "Nobody wants you."

Maria leaned forward. "Look, we need a plan. Any ideas, Cooper?"

"Why not just interview them and share what we find out?" Cooper replied. "Then we can decide what to do."

"Any other ideas, Jessie?" Maria drummed her fingers on the desk.

Jessie wasn't paying close attention. She wanted to ask Cooper about the dance she was creating. But she knew that if Cooper had the slightest idea that Jessie had watched her, the explosion that followed would flatten OPA.

"Cooper's right." Jessie paused. "These are grown people. They may be old, but like my grandmother, they definitely have minds of their own. Why not involve them in deciding what to do?"

"I think that Mrs. Lee would enjoy talking about her art and even showing her slides to our class," offered Julie.

Maria joined in. "My ladies love to talk. They have enough stories to last a year. I'll see what they want to do."

"Mr. Stinson is a professional musician. I'd like to do something with him. Him and me," said Cooper.

"I can't promise anything about Miss Harding," said Jessie. "But don't worry, I need that B."

Maria clapped her hands. "We've got a plan, Fours! So let's meet in a few days and see where we are. Then we can tell Mr. Reynolds."

On the way out, Mr. Reynolds stopped Jessie and Cooper.

"Here are your journals. At least we have a start," he said, "but I'd like a bit *more* for next week. Be assured that they are for my eyes only."

"But you said every two weeks!" protested Jessie.

Mr. Reynolds shook his head. "I changed my mind."

The two girls parted in the hall without speaking.

◇◇◇

In the theater, kids buzzed about like bees in a hive. Mr. Reynolds stood in front, his prompt book in hand. The loose-leaf binder held a copy of the script mounted on bigger, sturdier paper. This was the director's personal notebook jam-packed with notations and symbols. Jessie knew about this. She had been reading Mamatoo's prompt books from the time she was a little girl.

She knew the symbols for the movements—a language of initials, arrows, lines, abbreviations, and quick sketches. The director had to know where everyone moved, exactly when, and why. This was a blocking rehearsal where the actors practiced their positions as the play progressed.

Jessie dropped her book bag in a seat and ran up to join the others as they walked up to the stage. She knew where the chorus was supposed to be from scene to scene. When Jessie was on for her part as Harriet Tubman's younger sister Mary Ann, the chorus was offstage.

Six students made up the chorus. Jessie grinned. She was the only sixth-grader! Three eighth-grade boys and two seventh-grade girls had been chosen. Plus Jessie. Mamatoo had been right—this was a prize part.

The chorus was supposed to move as a single unit, turning from front to side to back. This required exact balance and poise. Jessie stood on the end nearest the audience. Like a wheel, the chorus moved through both acts.

Back in her seat, Jessie made notations on her script. As she reached into her book bag for a pen to underline areas she needed to focus on, the journal for Mr. Reynolds tumbled out onto the floor. Images of Cooper dancing came to her mind and helped her visualize the movements she had to make as part of the chorus.

Jessie sketched the movements of the chorus next to the directions. Acting involved more than getting up on a stage and being a character. Mamatoo had taught her that, and it seemed she had learned a lot from watching Cooper move, too.

"Hey, Jess," said Jamar, plopping down next to her. "I can't call you 'Red' anymore."

Self-conscious, Jessie touched her head to make sure the scarf was in place.

"Yeah, another 'Miss What-If' mistake," she said.

When he gave her a blank look, Jessie explained.

"That's what my family calls me. I should have let my hair alone. Now the color is awful. I look like the evil witch in *The Wizard of Oz*."

"Jess, I don't care about your hair. You have pretty hair. Listen, did you get into trouble with your Dad for going out with us to get some food?" asked Jamar.

"No, Dad didn't see me. But I don't like hiding anything from him, so I can't do it again." Jessie whispered the last part of the sentence, her face hot and flushed.

They sat quietly.

"That's OK. We can go to the cafeteria. There are plenty of vending machines there."

Jessie looked at Jamar. He meant what he said.

"Thanks, Jamar. Look, I've got to run to Evergreen for my Home Base project." Jessie grabbed her book bag, stuffing her script inside. "See you tomorrow?"

Jamar hesitated. "Jess, um . . . I, uh—I mean, are you going to the holiday dance?" he mumbled, obviously embarrassed.

Something in Jessie clicked. With a twirl she scooped up her book bag, "Now I am, if you are, Jamar." Shocked by her bravado, she rushed up the stairs and out of the theater.

◇◇◇

Miss Harding met Jessie in the hallway and led her straight to the kitchen. Jessie collapsed into a chair. The garden looked the same. So did the kitchen. But Miss Harding didn't. The same precise grace marked her movements. But something was different. In a flash, Jessie saw it.

"Where's your locket pin, Miss Harding? The beautiful gold one?" asked Jessie.

Miss Harding smiled a bit. "Right here in my pocket." She held the locket up, then placed it back in her pocket.

"Why aren't you wearing it?"

"I was, but I got a bit hot and took off my sweater."

By now Jessie knew enough about the elderly woman to realize that this answer was all she was going to get. The teakettle whistled.

"Headache today?" Miss Harding asked.

"No, I'm just tired and scared that I didn't pass two tests," admitted Jessie.

When Miss Harding lifted her eyebrows, Jessie continued.

"Being at OPA is exciting. I really want to be an actress, but my dad thinks I'm foolish. If I don't get all B's or better, he's going to make me leave OPA and go to a dull, stupid school," said Jessie, unable to stop. "And I dyed my hair. See?" Off came the scarf.

"We'll try a different tea and my banana nut bread today," was Miss Harding's response.

They sipped a pale red tea that smelled like cloves and cinnamon sticks. Jessie felt herself relax. It was like sitting with Mamatoo in her apartment and, like Mamatoo said, it was time to lay her cards on the table.

"Miss Harding, one of my grades depends on you. I don't want to interview anybody but you. I want to keep you, but I have to know more about you," said Jessie, forcing herself to look into Miss Harding's face.

There was no reply.

"I know that I don't have the right to interfere in your life. So, if you want me to leave you alone . . ." Jessie let the rest of the sentence share the air with the heady aroma of the tea.

"I have to think about this." Soft lines laced the woman's face. Today her hair was braided and wound around her head, like a silver crown. It was easy to see that at one time Miss Harding had been beautiful. But the same pain Jessie had seen before filled Miss Harding's eyes like a guest that just refused to leave.

Jessie knew she must persevere. If she had made a habit of giving up, she would never have won a place at OPA, or a part in the play. Or met the Fours. Or danced with Jamar. Or dyed her hair red, then black. Or met this unusual woman who revealed so little of herself.

"Courage," Jessie told herself.

"Look, Miss Harding, are you famous or something?" she asked, taking a stab in the dark.

"Yes, I am, Jessie," said Miss Harding calmly.

Stunned, Jessie knocked her mug over. She set it right, glad that it was empty.

"I was an actress. I had another name—Corrine James."

"Corrine James!" Jessie repeated, awestruck. "My grandmother talks about you. I've seen your name in some of her books." Jessie paused. "But why are you living here, under another name?"

"I needed to live a more private life."

Jessie had a million questions. "Can I interview you? Do you have any of your movies here? Do you have a scrapbook? Or any playbills? Can I tell my grandmother about you? And my dad?"

"So many questions at once! But, I like you, Jessie Williams, no matter what color your hair is." Miss Harding chuckled. "And yes, you may tell your family who I am."

Jessie nodded. "Would you consider talking to some students in the acting department at OPA?"

"Perhaps. It has been many years since I've spoken as an actress."

Jessie grinned from ear to ear. "What a day! I finally found my own living treasure!"

The elderly woman looked at the garden and sighed. "Have you, Jessie?"

The minute Jessie got home, she ran downstairs and hit her grandmother's buzzer. One long and three short.

"I've missed you, Jessie, my dear. We pass one another like ships in the night. I'm at the theater and you're at OPA," said Mamatoo.

Jessie perched on a stool by the kitchen counter, while Mamatoo prepared a soup.

"Mamatoo, I have something unbelievable to tell you," said Jessie, barely containing her excitement.

"Well, it's about time," replied Mamatoo, with a broad smile. Her eyes sparkled with curiosity.

"Do you know a Miss Laura Harding?" asked Jessie.

"Isn't she the secretive lady you've been trying to talk to at the home? The one who owns the place?"

"Yes . . . and no," replied Jessie.

"What does that mean?" asked Mamatoo.

"Mamatoo, Miss Harding is really Corrine James! She just told me this afternoon." Jessie waited for her grandmother's response, but Mamatoo didn't move. Had she heard?

A second later, Mamatoo straightened up and whistled, a long, impressed whistle. "Corrine James, the actress?"

"Yes, the very same!" said Jessie, nearly tumbling off her stool. "And she said I could tell the family. But she is a very private person."

Mamatoo's face darkened a little. "Ah, with every right to be private." Jessie could see a small storm brewing in her grandmother's face. "Jessie, that woman is one of the greatest stage and film actresses of all times. If she'd been white, the world would have sat at her feet. But being an African-American cut her off from that kind of fame." Mamatoo slammed a pot down on the stove and poured in homemade broth. "To think that she ended up in some old folks' home. That's enough to make me blow a fuse."

When Mamatoo got started there was no stopping her. Jessie watched as her grandmother sliced onions and diced celery, carrots, peppers, and squash.

Mamatoo grabbed a big spoon and stirred the veggies so fast, Jessie could swear she heard them spinning. This would be some vegetable soup!

"The great Corrine James! Hidden away in that place alone! That's what has my dander up, Jessie," said Mamatoo, turning around.

"Mamatoo, she *owns* Evergreen Residential Home. And she lives with her friends."

Her grandmother virtually glared at Jessie.

"OK," said Jessie, "you're right, there's a sad part about that—about her. Maybe I should invite her to dinner."

"Now you've got your thinking cap on. But we have to honor her privacy." Mamatoo was rolling again. "I wonder if she would be willing to come to the theater? We should have a revival of her films. I know there are videotapes of her stage plays. No, I'm getting ahead of myself. This requires careful thought." Jessie's grandmother mused, stirring the bubbling soup. That was the end of the conversation about Corrine James.

Abruptly, Mamatoo said, "Jessie, take that miserable scarf off your head! I know you think your hair looks terrible. Well, you're right. It does."

Shocked, Jessie opened her mouth. At first nothing came out, then only squeaks. "Mamatoo! How could you say that to me?"

Mamatoo reached over the counter and snatched the scarf off Jessie's head. "Because it's the truth and you know it. Don't expect me to lie to you. Now, I bought two herbal rinses for this latest 'Miss What-If' disaster, and we're going to use them tonight. Go add some wood to the fire. I need a cup of tea for fortitude."

By the time Jessie left her grandmother's apartment, her hair looked better. The first herbal rinse reduced the harsh jet black color. The second rinse gave her hair some life and body. Mamatoo had cut two inches off. Together they had tossed the scarf into the fire.

In her room, Jessie finished her homework. Cass was on the phone. Cass had never failed tests or brought home low grades. Sometimes Jessie wondered if her older sister just knew what was going to happen next—at least when it came to school—and was always ready. And for Dad, nobody beat Cass in the smart and pretty department, except Mom.

Jessie exhaled. There was one more chore to attend to. The journal for Mr. Reynolds. Carefully she surveyed her multitude of colored pens. Today felt like a dark gray pen. Cass hung up the phone.

Lying across the bed in her pajamas, Cass yawned. Her books were stacked like blocks. Even her clothes for tomorrow were hung out neatly with matching shoes, jewelry, and hair ribbons. Cass changed her bed every four days with matching sheets and pillow shams, bed ruffles, and comforters. *If* Jessie remembered, and that was a big if, her bed might get changed every week or so with whatever she snatched from the linen closet.

Jessie grinned. A few months ago she'd grabbed a green flannel bottom sheet, a red and yellow striped top sheet, and two purple silky pillowcases from the linen closet. Cass had almost fainted! In return for borrowing Cass's gold chain necklace, Jessie had allowed Cass to remake her bed in daffodil sheets, pillowcases, and shams that matched her own.

"Jessie, it's been ten days since you changed your bed," said Cass, climbing under her freshly changed sheets of pastel plaid and matching comforter.

"Who's counting?" Jessie asked. "To tell the truth, I have so much on my mind, the last thing I care about is sheets." She opened her journal.

Cass groaned, long and loud. "Do you want me to change them for you?"

The idea of sleeping in matching tulips, rose gardens, or lilies of the valley was enough to make Jessie gag. Why not sheets with wild animals, famous actresses, or answers to sixth-grade pop math exams?

"If you have to, but I can't stand flowers! Daffodils drive me crazy!"

"Fine," said Cass. "Hey, Mamatoo worked a miracle on your hair!"

Jessie glanced up in surprise. "How did you know?"

Cass smiled. "I went with her to buy the rinses. It was a gift for you. I knew it would work!"

"Thanks. I promised not to do anything to my hair other than wash, dry, roll, brush, oil, and comb it," Jessie admitted.

"That's called damage control. Sleep good, little sister." Cass turned over on her side. Jessie turned her three-way lightbulb down to the lowest setting and thought about what to write in the journal. Mr. Reynolds said he wanted more. There were the sketches. Jessie wrote:

> Dear Mr. Reynolds,
>
> I saw Cooper dance. She didn't know I was there. I don't want her to find out. She moved like wind and fire and tears. It was her own private dance. It was beautiful. That's all I can say.
>
> P. S. I sketched her dancing. Remember, this is our secret.

Jessie lay back against the pillows, the journal open on her lap. Seeing Cooper dance and meeting Corrine James, all in the past twenty-four hours. What a day!

Her bedroom door was open. She could hear her father and mother—their voices blended, rising and falling as one. Cass snored lightly. Jessie knew Mamatoo would be either reading in front of the fireplace or asleep. Jessie soon fell asleep herself.

Fierce winds woke Jessie in the middle of the night. They blew against the house. Soft light from the hallway meshed with the semi-darkness of the bedroom. Jessie reached for her favorite stuffed animal—a giraffe. She nestled under her covers and tucked it under her chin.

Images of Cooper dancing the tragic story of Addie Mae Collins flitted across her mind, mixed with worries about the two tests she had taken earlier that day. Like a refrain, the golden locket pin and the sad-eyed lady who wore it drifted by. Finally, Jessie slept.

◇◇◇

The following weekend, Jessie managed to make one more trip to see Miss Harding. But the actress was not willing to commit to an appearance at OPA.

The tests had proven to be disasters. Despite her pleas, the teachers did not relent. No extra makeup work. She simply had to study and apply herself. There was no alternative.

Jessie fell into a deep funk. It wasn't that she wasn't studying. She was. Just not enough. With the play, the "Living Treasures" project, and running to see Cooper dance, how could any sane person expect her to get—at least—straight B's?

Dad did.

During math class on Monday afternoon, a solution came to her. Jessie's mind leapt from one strategy to another, until finally she decided that it just might be possible to manage an end run around her father.

That night, Jessie put her plan into action. Every night Dad came home more exhausted than the night before. Because John was out with the flu, there was too much to do at the store. Kwanzaa and Christmas books kept arriving by the box loads.

"Books and books and more books!" said Mr. Williams, coughing as he took off his coat.

"Honey, if you don't take it easy, that cough could turn into pneumonia," said Mrs. Williams. "The store will survive. Don't kill yourself."

Jessie peeked over her math book. Doing her homework publicly in front of the entire family for lengthy periods of time was the first step. She called it the "Do and die" plan. If Dad saw her putting in hundreds of hours studying, how could he send her to Milton? She knew that Mom would argue for the value of trying and working hard.

"Hi, Dad." Jessie stuck her pencil behind her ear. She figured that made her look studious.

Mr. Williams stopped and stared, "You're hitting the books? What's happening to you, Jessie? I've never seen you work this hard on schoolwork!"

Jessie reached down and added two heavy books to the stack on the table. This was the "Tons of thick books" strategy. As an actress, she knew how valuable appearances could be. She'd gone to the library and taken out fifteen books on math, history, science, and literature. Nothing on acting. Jessie smiled inside at the image she presented: Jessie Williams, serious, committed student, surrounded by very, very thick books.

Reaching for a new gigantic pink eraser, Jessie said, "Dad, I've given some thought to what you've been saying. I want you to know that I am dedicated to being a good student."

"I never thought I'd live to hear those words." Her father leaned back in his reclining chair.

"See, Dad, there's hope for me." Jessie grinned as she went back to work.

While Mom bustled about heating dinner and fussing at her husband, Jessie labored. Cass was working on the computer downstairs. According to the plan, Jessie had to do her computer work in the library so she could maximize her public study time at home. How could Dad or Mom see how hard she was studying if she was hidden away in the bedroom downstairs?

Working furiously, Jessie didn't stop until her parents went to bed. That was another part of the plan, called "Never fall asleep on the job!" Faithfully, she executed the plan every night that week.

◇◇◇

During rehearsal on Friday, the chorus got stuck. While Harriet journeyed back and forth nineteen times from the South to the North to free her family and three hundred other slaves, Mr. Reynolds wanted the chorus to move in a half-circle swing as they chanted. The chant was done in combinations. First the boys, then the girls, followed by mixed pairs, and then the whole group. For Jessie, the chanting and two-step slide merged together as one. But she had practiced whenever she could squeeze a second away from her "Do and die" regimen.

The chorus chant was, "Running, running, running. Always hiding. Always moving. Running, running, running." The members of the chorus stumbled over their feet, bumping into each other.

"What can I do to help you feel this?" asked Mr. Reynolds, his voice calm and slow. "Getting this sequence right is about feeling the rhythm of the chant. Once you feel the beat of the chant and the beat of the move, and put it with the beat of Harriet going back and forth across the stage, you're home free."

Bewildered, the chorus continued to collide with one another.

"Jessie, you've got it. I want everybody to see and hear what this part feels like. Sylvia, you're on. Don't worry about mistakes. Just try to stay with the flow. You're Harriet now. Everyone else, watch Jessie." He put his hands up, then dropped them.

Jessie wanted to hide. But when Mr. Reynolds spoke, she obeyed. Walking forward, she stopped. Cooper was in the third row! Closing her eyes and breathing slowly, Jessie focused her attention on what she had to do.

As Sylvia began to make her way across the stage, as if she was being hunted, Jessie started the chant. Timing the syllables of the chant to Sylvia's steps, she began the set of movements. In her mind, Jessie visualized what she was doing. The power of the chant and the play took over. Jessie loved being lost in the flow of the play.

Her body knew when to stop. It took a couple of seconds to refocus. Out of the corner of her eye, Jessie tried to see the reaction of the rest of the chorus members. Individually, they were going through the chant.

Mr. Reynolds waved his arms in the air. "That's it, chorus! Work on it by yourselves, then I'll call you together to practice as a group. Once you get this one, the other chants and songs will make sense. Thank you, Jessie."

The grin on Jessie's face spread from one end of the stage to the other. A thank you from her teacher equaled a dozen roses and three curtain calls! Jamar grinned at her. She watched Cooper get up, walk to the door, and stand there.

One of the chorus members touched Jessie's arm. Jessie turned around. Amazed, she realized that her fellow chorus members wanted to learn from her. So she taught them for the next half hour. When she checked the door again, Cooper was gone.

"Listen, Jessie, want to stop in the cafeteria with the rest of us after rehearsal?" asked Jamar, suddenly by her side.

"Sure. But I can't stay long. I've got homework for days."

"Me too," Jamar said.

Most of the chorus and principal actors trekked to the cafeteria. Here she was again, sitting next to Jamar among seventh and eighth graders! And the compliments on her performance kept coming. She felt like a real member of the cast.

While the kids talked and teased one another, Jessie thought, "OPA is the best school in the world! Imagine, me, Jessie Williams, here! I wish Mrs. Grant could see me now. No, I don't. I know I'm here. That's enough."

Time ran out too quickly. Jessie left, waving to her new acting friends. And Jamar. She'd told him she was going to Evergreen. But as Jessie walked down the hallway, she altered her course.

Tiptoeing and holding her book bag close to her body was easy. The hard part was sneaking into the theater without attracting Cooper's attention. That meant opening the door without making a sound.

Bracing herself, Jessie gently pulled the door toward her. She slipped into the theater without a sound. Willing herself invisible, Jessie eased into the closest seat.

The music from Cooper's cassette recorder wafted through the air. This music was new. Not gospel music, but deep down make-you-want-to-cry blues from a single guitar. Dad loved the blues. Jessie had heard blues music for as long as she could remember. But this guitar player was new to her. Jessie leaned back in her seat and watched the magic that Cooper created when she danced the story of her name.

"When Cooper dances," Jessie thought, "she gets centered in the dance the same way I do when I act. People call it getting lost, but Mamatoo calls it getting found. And it *is* like finding yourself—your unique self." She took out her sketch pad and pencils. Frantically, she tried to capture Cooper's movements, one flowing into the next.

When Cooper packed up and left the stage, Jessie hurried out. If she rushed, she might manage a quick visit with Miss Harding. Without warning, she rounded a corner, and ran right into Cooper.

"What are you doing here?" Cooper placed a hand on her hip.

Jessie called on her acting ability. "I thought you might have a late class or practice."

"I gave you my schedule. Those are the only times I dance here!" said Cooper. Wrapped in thread to keep her straight hair tight, dozens of braids hung below Cooper's shoulders. Today she wore black jeans, black leather boots, a black "Free Huey Newton" sweatshirt, and her usual litany of political buttons.

Jessie sighed. More than anything, she wanted to ask Cooper about her dance and the blues music, but she could never do that. She could never tell Cooper what a talented dancer she was.

"Look, Cooper, I'm supposed to watch you dance and you have to watch me act. So stop hassling me! You going to Evergreen?" Jessie changed the subject and started walking.

"Nope. I've got to get home. I'll go tomorrow."

When they reached the front door, a heavy thunderstorm struck. Rain poured down in sheets. Dismayed,

Jessie sat down on the floor and stared at the metal-gray sky. Cooper joined her, while a few students drifted by with umbrellas.

"It has to slack off soon. We might as well wait it out." Jessie reached into her bag and took out an apple. "Want a bite?"

Cooper shook her head.

"When I was little, I didn't know where rain came from," said Jessie, watching the rain. "I thought and thought. Then I announced to my family, like I was some kind of rain expert, that the sky had holes in it and the rain water leaked through."

Jessie laughed and bit into the apple.

Cooper's eyes widened. Then the shadow of a smile crossed her face.

"What did you think, Cooper?" asked Jessie. "About where rain came from?"

Cooper leaned forward and crossed her legs. Her thin face seemed so stressed and strained. For the first time, Jessie noticed blotches under her eyes.

"I didn't think much about the rain when I was real young. I loved the stars. I thought they were rhinestones. My mother had rhinestone earrings." Cooper smiled at the memory.

Jessie nodded.

The silence moved between them.

Cooper shifted. "But when I did think about rain, I

told myself when it rained, the stars were crying. I called rain 'star tears.' "

Jessie shook her head. "That's beautiful. I like yours better than mine."

"I like yours. It's funny." Cooper got up. "You saved that chorus. You knew exactly what to do."

Unsure of what to do, Jessie also stood up. How could she tell this complicated girl what a fine dancer she was? The regular classes and practices demonstrated Cooper's work and discipline, but her own composition revealed her unique talents. "Thanks. I think you should be in the first line and dance solo." Somehow that wasn't enough.

Jessie took a deep breath. "You're so good, Chuki."

A wry smile played on Cooper's face. She pushed the door open, turned around, and said, "Thanks, Williams."

By the time Jessie reached Evergreen, she was dripping wet. Miss Harding was at the door. "Jessie, I thought we'd meet in my room today. You can dry yourself off."

Jessie nodded. She felt like a wet noodle. As she followed Miss Harding, Jessie reviewed her manners: talk calmly, no matter what; listen and smile; don't stare at anything. What would Miss Harding's room look like?

Furtively, Jessie checked to make sure she'd brought her cassette recorder and camera. Two bulges in the middle of her book bag told her they were both there. She hoped that she'd get enough information to catch up with the rest of the Fours.

Jessie gasped when Miss Harding opened the door. The place was overflowing with flowers. Jessie counted seven bouquets. Red poppies, white and yellow mums, orchids, hollyhocks, and lilies that looked as soft as velvet.

It was a small apartment, with a living room, dining area, kitchen, and hallway with a couple of open doors. But the life of the apartment was on the walls. Photographs of Corrine James, the woman Jessie knew as Laura Harding, and other celebrities of her time, hung next to framed theater and movie posters. Jessie toured the room, reading every single autograph and line of print.

Photographs of famous playwrights, writers, and actors—Langston Hughes, Richard Wright, Ruby Dee, Canada Lee, James Baldwin, Lena Horne, Ossie Davis, Amiri Baraka, Harry Belafonte, and dozens more—caught her attention. Their autograph notes to Corrine James were personal and often lengthy. These were people she knew well and who admired her!

Jessie stepped back so she could take in the large framed play posters. Many of the plays she recognized from Mamatoo's books about African-American theater. Every three years or so, Mamatoo selected three plays from the past, and the repertory company put on a series called, "Goin' Home." Jessie had seen one series which included *Mamba's Daughter, Our Lan,* and *Anna Lucasta.*

Posters for all three of those were up, plus at least twelve others, with Miss Harding in the lead.

Over on the far wall was a photograph she didn't expect to find: Judith Jamison. Cooper's idol!

"You know Judith Jamison?" asked Jessie.

"Yes, I do."

Jessie smiled. "Do you know her well? I mean do you still know her?"

"Why?"

"Because this girl I know—you've seen her, Addie Mae Cooper, the dancer—she loves Judith Jamison!"

"Yes, I've known Judy for many years. We have remained close friends."

Filing that information away in her mind, Jessie returned to one of the questions that gnawed at her. "Should I call you Miss James?"

Instead of answering, the elderly woman handed her a fluffy peach towel and took her book bag.

"Take that wet jacket off. I need a cup of hot chocolate and so do you."

Gazing around, Jessie wiped her face and neck. Simple wood furniture, a comfortable couch, and African art and sculpture decorated the apartment. On the coffee table Jessie spotted several scrapbooks. It was difficult to resist the temptation to open them. But she managed. Rules were rules. Like Mamatoo said, "If there wasn't a darn good reason for a rule, no one would pay any attention to it."

"Jessie, come sit here," offered Miss Harding.

The dining area was by a picture window that faced the garden. For some minutes they sat in comfortable silence, sipping their hot chocolate.

"My real name is Laura Harding. My stage name was Corrine James. Call me by my true name," she said, the locket pin shining on the brown collar of her dress.

"Which did you like better, being in the movies or the theater?"

Miss Harding smiled. "The theater gave me my life as an actress."

"What was it like? Knowing all these famous actors. Being in these great plays. How did you get started?" asked Jessie. "Would you mind if I tape-recorded our talk? Please."

"Yes, you may. I trust your discretion."

Quickly, Jessie took her cassette recorder out and turned it on. She gestured to Miss Harding to continue.

"I started in the early 1940s. I went to Hunter College in New York and worked. I joined A.N.T., the American Negro Theater, and did odd jobs and bit parts. My first real role was in the A.N.T. version of the musical *South Pacific.*

"A.N.T. like ant?" asked Jessie.

Miss Harding smiled, "How perceptive of you! Frederick O'Neal, A.N.T.'s founder, expected us to work like ants. In 1944, we had our first major hit with—"

"The play *Anna Lucasta,*" interrupted Jessie. "And it played 956 performances on Broadway!"

"My, Jessie Williams, you certainly know your theater lore. Right. So overnight we went from busy ants to thundering elephants. From there I went through plays and movies like a wagon on fire. Then it stopped. Or rather, I stopped the wagon," said Miss Harding.

"Why? Did something bad happen?" Jessie watched Miss Harding touch the locket pin.

"Yes. I got so obsessed with being the first black actress to make it big, I lost what mattered—my own love of the craft and the one person who always loved me." Miss Harding's voice trembled.

"And the locket pin?" Jessie asked as gently as she could.

"A gift from my mother. Her initials are engraved on it. It contains the last photo of my mother, Alma, and me. Mama died in a hospital without me there. Her only child. I was too busy finishing some stupid movie. I still can't forgive myself," said the sad-eyed lady.

Jessie thought long and hard. Mamatoo said that making mistakes was just part of being human. "If your mama loved you, Miss Harding, and I bet she did, then she forgives you, and I know God forgives you. I go overboard all the time and get so wrapped up in acting I forget about everything else—that is, until my Dad reminds me."

Miss Harding smiled a bit. "Jessie Williams, you are certainly wise for your age. Well, now you know more about me than most people do."

"I won't tell anyone." Jessie reached for the cassette

recorder, took out the tape, and tossed it in a nearby wastebasket. "May I see the picture of your mother?"

Miss Harding handed Jessie the locket and walked away. Carefully, Jessie opened the tiny latch. In the tiny picture, Miss Harding's mother was hugging her daughter and smiling. Alma appeared to be frail.

Quietly, Miss Harding sat back down at the table. "These are for you, Jessie, to help you prepare for your presentation." She handed Jessie the scrapbooks that had been lying on the coffee table. "If you'd like, I'll talk with the students in the acting department. And I would certainly enjoy meeting your family. I know about your grandmother. In fact, I attended the opening night of her play recently. You should be very proud of her."

Jessie laid the locket down and gratefully took the three albums. "You were there?" asked Jessie in surprise.

Miss Harding nodded.

Jessie ran her hand over the stack of scrapbooks. "Thank you, Miss Harding. I'll guard these with my life."

Chuckling, Miss Harding handed Jessie another dry towel. "Believe me, they're not worth your life. Look, the rain has stopped."

◇◇◇

Twenty minutes later, instead of heading home, Jessie was on a bus bound for her father's bookstore. A smile creased the corner of her mouth.

"I've got my notebook, plenty of pencils, erasers, and

schoolbooks. And three great albums of the career of a legend. Dad will be so proud when he sees me doing research in the bookstore. He'll smile at me the same way he did at Cooper," reasoned Jessie.

Practically bouncing, Jessie held the door of the bookstore open for a customer, then strolled in. Customers milled in the aisles. At the counter, Margaret was ringing up some purchases and answering a young man's questions. But where was Dad?

There he was. Standing next to him, unloading a box of newly arrived books, was Cooper! Grinning up at her father. Touching the brand-new books that belonged to her family. Acting like she belonged here. When Jessie saw Cass coming out of the Author Room, she imploded. Her sister, the traitor!

"Jess! I just got here. Joe's in the back," said Cass, winding her hair in a knot and pinning it back. "I figured Dad might need some help. Mom's right. He's been working too hard. What are you doing here?"

Fifty answers ran through Jessie's head. Nothing came out, just sputters.

"Jess, is something wrong?"

"Cass, how could you? How could you do this to me?"

Suddenly, Cass threw her hands up. "This is about Chuki Cooper being here, isn't it? Jessie, I just got here. I walked in and there she was. Let's find out what's going on. Follow my lead. And don't, and I mean *don't*, lose your temper. Don't open your mouth!"

Snatched by the wrist, Jessie stumbled behind Cass.

"Hey, Dad! What's up?" Cass said. "I see you've got some unexpected help."

"Cass! Jess? What are you doing here?" asked Mr. Williams.

Cass stepped closer to the counter and held out her hand, talking in one steady syrupy sweet stream: "You're Chuki Cooper. I hope I got your name right. Jess has told me so much about you. I'm Cass, her sister. What are you doing here?"

Jessie grinned inside at the flush that started at Cooper's neck and spread across her face. Cass could spin out twenty things in one sentence. Even Mr. Williams had been shushed.

"I stopped by to look at some books," Cooper said, her voice low, but defiant.

Cass wedged her body between Jessie and the counter. "Then how did you get back there? The books are out here."

Cooper looked at Mr. Williams, but he was busy. Without warning, Joe came up.

"Joe," continued Cass, without missing a beat. "Help Dad while Chuki, Jess, and I work in the Author Room." Cass ushered the two girls to the seclusion and quiet of the back room.

Cass stood by the door. She wasn't about to leave these two wildcats unsupervised. "You two sit over there. Talk this out. I don't want Dad upset, so keep your voices low. And Jess—"

"Cass, I know, don't lose my temper."

Cooper and Jessie sat across the round table from each other. Cass stood guard.

Jessie began. "Cooper, I want to know what you're doing here working in the store. You said you were going home!"

Cooper sighed. "I was, but at the last minute I decided not to."

"Why?" Jessie asked, feeling her anger surge.

"Because I'm tired of going home to an empty, dark place with a mother who's never there and a father who never calls. And this place is warm and friendly and full of books I love."

Jessie pressed harder. "And my Dad is warm and friendly and thinks you're wonderful. Right, Cooper?"

"So we're back to Cooper. A little while ago it was Chuki," said Cooper. "Yeah, your father is nice."

"Well, he's *my* father! I don't want you in this store ever again. You hear that? Spend time with your own father and leave mine alone! This is my family! Get your own!" warned Jessie, the anger swooping out of her mouth like a fierce hawk diving for its kill. She ignored Cass's shocked expression and the sick knot in her own stomach.

Things got worse, fast. Tears welled up in Cooper's eyes and spilled over, falling down her face. Her long braids cascaded around her face. Sobbing, she held her head in her hands. Desperate, Jessie looked toward her sister for help. But Cass's face was grim.

Jessie leaned over and whispered, "Look, Chuki, stop crying. Please."

Cooper laid her head down and continued to cry.

"Listen, Chuki, I'm sorry. What I said was wrong. OK, it was mean. Look, I know somebody who is a good friend of Judith Jamison," said Jessie, touching the girl.

That didn't work. Cass was suddenly at Cooper's side.

"Hey, come on," whispered Cass, patting Cooper's shoulder. "It's tough when your parents aren't there for you. It feels like they don't love you anymore. Most of the time they do, Chuki. But they get overwhelmed by their own lives. That happens to our dad."

"What do you know about having a father abandon you? Your dad adores you!" retorted Cooper.

Curious, Jessie waited for her sister's response.

"There was a time when Dad was gone most of the time. He even missed my birthday party and Thanksgiving," Cass admitted. "Jessie was real little. Every night I cried myself to sleep. But I hid the way I felt from him and took it out on my mother. It was bad."

Cooper sat up and wiped at her face. Her chest heaved. Every now and then a sob would escape.

"You understand," she said, taking in gulps of air. "It hurts so much."

Cass gripped Cooper's shoulders. Jessie was in shock. What was Cass talking about? When did Dad ever miss her birthday or any family holiday? But Jessie would have to sort that out later.

Right now, Jessie felt terrible. What she'd said to Cooper was awful! She'd been mean and cruel, just like Mrs. Grant. The thought of having acted like Mrs. Grant was worse than any punishment she could imagine. What could she do? She thought about what Mrs. Grant should have done. Determined, Jessie took the plunge.

"Chuki, what I said was wrong and mean. I'm not like that," said Jessie, aware of Cass's raised eyebrows and Cooper's bleak eyes. "I'm sorry for what I said. I just want my dad to smile at me the way he does at you. I can't do anything to please him. He doesn't even want me working here. But he wants you here. I apologize for being mean."

"Honest?" asked Cooper.

Jessie held out her hand. "Honest."

Cooper wiped her nose. "OK. So who knows Judith Jamison?"

"Wait a minute, not so fast," said Cass. "Jessie, you need to talk to Dad."

Clutching her hands in her lap, Jessie stared at the edge of the table. Cooper started to get up, but Cass pulled her down.

The expression on Cass's face forced both girls to pay close attention. "Don't move. Listen, this might help you, Chuki. Jess, this thing with Dad is bad for you. Look at the way you treated Chuki! That person saying those cruel words wasn't my sister."

Tears now filled Jessie's eyes. Cass was right. But facing Dad was out of the question. Absolutely, totally out of the question.

"Cass, how can I talk to Dad? He never listens to me, unless I'm slaving over homework," said Jessie.

"Hey." Mr. Williams appeared at the door. "I need your help! All three of you!" he said, running his fingers through his hair.

One swift look flew from girl to girl. In one motion they stood up, erasing from their faces every sign of what had happened between them. Cass led the way.

For the next two hours, everyone worked nonstop. Cass and Margaret took turns handling the cash register. Joe unpacked boxes of books while Jessie inventoried them. Cooper placed books on the shelves and answered questions, leading customers to their desired selections.

In preparation for that night's author reading and signing, Jessie set up the Author Room. There would be lots of fans tonight, so she crammed in extra chairs. August Wilson, the Tony Award–winning playwright, was world-renowned and a close friend of Mr. Williams's. A deluxe gift edition of his plays had just been published. After his reading, the autographing would be done at a table up front.

A rectangular table, large enough for two people, stood in a back corner. Ducking around customers, Jessie tugged it over next to the counter, then placed two chairs behind it. On the table she set a pitcher of ice water and a glass, several black pens, and a pad of paper. Margaret would sit with Mr. Wilson, writing down the inscriptions people wanted, so the author could easily copy them. Finally, Jessie was done.

Cass wiped her brow. "I'm beat! Jess, I called Mom and told her we were at the store. And I had Chuki call home."

"Did you get your mother?" asked Jessie.

Cooper nodded. "Yeah. She didn't care. Look, I'm going to grab my things and head home. Thanks."

Jessie shook her head. "Are you crazy? It's late and dark outside. If you have to go home now, Joe can take you. Right, Cass?"

"Sure," said Cass, Joe's program director.

"Or you can stay, eat with us, and hear Mr. Wilson. Then we'll take you home," offered Jessie.

The gratitude in Cooper's eyes shamed Jessie.

"OK," she said. "I'd love to meet Mr. Wilson. I've got money to pay for my own food."

Mr. Williams leaned over the counter. "This dinner is on me. Small payment for your help! Joe, take orders for dinner! We have just enough time before the program begins."

Later, during the reception for Mr. Wilson, Jessie saw a familiar figure at the back of the room. It was Miss Harding! Acting on impulse, she eased close to the soft-spoken playwright and pointed to the back. His eyes widened in amazement.

"Jessie, is that Corrine James?" he murmured.

"Yes, but she's really shy," Jessie responded.

Mr. Wilson nodded. "Excuse me."

He walked to the back of the room. For the next half hour, he and Miss Harding conversed. Then she left, actually grinning!

"What happened?" Jessie asked him.

Jessie was rewarded with a cryptic smile from the famous black playwright. "Jessie, you may have helped make theater history tonight. Only time will tell."

After the store emptied and everything was back in its proper place, Jessie waved good-bye to Margaret and watched until she was safely in her car. Joe and Cass left for a party. Dad, Jessie, and Cooper locked up.

Exhausted, Jessie, Cooper, and Mr. Williams climbed in the van. When they arrived at Cooper's apartment building, she jumped out and Jessie ran after her.

"Thanks, Chuki," Jessie said.

Cooper turned around. In the streetlight her face looked thin and wan.

"What your sister said was true. I did learn something from listening to her talk to you. I need to talk to my father, too. At least he'd know how I feel," she said, her voice soft and slow.

Cooper walked away. On the way to the van, Jessie peered up. The windows in Cooper's apartment were dark.

◇◇◇

At rehearsal Saturday morning, Jessie listened carefully to Mr. Reynolds. Jamar sat next to her. Sylvia, as Harriet, and a group of escaping slaves were on stage. The rest of the cast paid close attention.

"Know where you are and who you are. You are slaves willing to bet your lives on the chance of making it from North Carolina to Canada. Your mothers and fathers have been sold away from you. Even your children. Running for freedom—that's your whole life now. You're cold, hungry, tired, and scared to death," he said, pacing up and down. "Dogs might get you or snakes in the woods. Harriet knows the way; but she's tough and she's got that gun."

Quiet laughter followed his last sentence. Everyone knew that Harriet Tubman had sometimes used her big gun to force scared runaways to continue.

The group aligned themselves for the scene. Furtively, they ran across the stage, from upstage left to downstage front. They huddled in a circle.

"We rest here. No fire," said Harriet Tubman.

Some of the runaways complained and argued with her.

Harriet stood up, her hand on the gun at her waist. "You runs with me like I tell you or you dies. We got to keep goin.'"

Chills ran up Jessie's spine.

"Jess, you are coming to the holiday dance, aren't you?" Jamar whispered. Dressed in jeans, running shoes, and a cable-knit sweater, he looked more like a teenage model than a junior-high school kid. Jessie wondered if he ever thought about how handsome he was. She didn't think so. His mind was on school, acting, college, and becoming a United States Senator.

"And my mind is going to stay on my grades at OPA, Dad, the projects for Mr. Reynolds, Cooper, and not losing my temper!" she vowed to herself.

"The holiday dance?" she asked vaguely.

"The one next Friday. Jess, what's on your mind?" he asked.

With a rueful smile, Jessie replied, "Jamar, believe me, you don't want to know. I'll probably be there."

"Don't dye your hair for the dance, Jess. I like you the way you are," he said, getting up to go onstage.

"I wish I did," murmured Jessie.

After rehearsal ended, Jessie checked the dance theater for Cooper. She wasn't there. Jessie peeked into the door window of each practice room. Identical rooms with smooth wooden floors, long walls covered with equally long mirrors, and practice bars on the opposite side.

There were dancers, but none of them was Cooper. For a while Jessie hung around. Disappointed, she finally headed home.

On Sunday night, Jessie organized her sketches of Cooper dancing. One by one she put them in sequence, numbered, and dated them. She secured them in an envelope and placed it in back of the journal. It was time for another entry.

Dear Mr. Reynolds,

I was mean to Cooper. I apologized, but I feel bad. I have to stop losing my temper. Yesterday, I tried to see Cooper dance, but she wasn't there. I really wanted to see her dance. How can I like her dancing and get so mad and jealous? It doesn't make sense. Here are the sketches. You can see for yourself. That's all.

After closing the journal, Jessie lay back against the pillows. Across the room, Cass prepared for bed.

"Cass, are you mad at me?" asked Jessie.

"No. Disappointed," said Cass, holding a roller in one hand. "Jess, Chuki's no threat to you. Is it because she's light-skinned? Because she dresses super black? Because Dad likes her?"

"Try all of the above," admitted Jessie.

Cass carefully wound a lock of hair around a roller. "That girl is unhappy, lonely, afraid, and doesn't feel like she belongs anywhere. Only in the bookstore can she pretend that she's part of a real family."

"I didn't think about that," mumbled Jessie.

Cass let out a sigh. "I respect her. She manages to get herself to school and do well. From what you say, Chuki is very disciplined. With nobody caring about them, most girls in her shoes would be in trouble."

"I never thought about her that way," Jessie echoed herself.

In a clear, strong voice Cass went on, "It's time you started thinking straight about some important stuff, Jessie."

◇◇◇

In Home Base on Monday morning, the Fours convened. It was still difficult for Jessie to meet Cooper's gaze. She kept hearing Cass's words. Jessie slumped back and listened to Maria.

"I've got photos and an interview with both sisters on tape. They said they'd be 'pleased as plums' to come to class and talk about their lives, reported Maria. What about you, Julie?"

Julie twisted a strand of her hair. "Mrs. Lee is nervous about doing anything big. But she said she will come to class and talk."

"Mr. Stinson and I are working on ours. I'll let you know," said Cooper.

Jessie spoke up. "Miss Harding will let me know when she'll come to class."

"We'd better let Mr. Reynolds know what we're doing," said Maria, getting up.

A brief explanation to Mr. Reynolds and straight answers to his questions earned his approval.

"Success!" Maria reported back to the group.

Julie spoke up. "You know, we used to go to Evergreen together. We don't anymore. I miss going together. I don't feel like we're a group anymore. Maria, you worry about grades. Same with you, Jessie. Chuki, you have to make the first dance line or else. I'm no better with my family and the fire. But all we do is worry by ourselves. We're not the Fours. We're four single, separate Ones."

"Remember when we went to the back-to-school dance? We were terrified. Jessie, you had to make Julie stay! Chuki sure had fun. My folks surrounded me like a moat around a castle, but we were together," Maria said in a faraway voice.

Cooper stirred. "I know I complained about our shows for the seniors at Evergreen. But it felt good to do our stuff together and hear them clapping for us. Now we don't do anything together."

Jessie said, "True. But what do we do about it? We've each got regular classes, practice classes, homework, and projects."

"We could meet once a week somewhere. Like the cafeteria," suggested Julie.

"I don't have time for extra meetings," said Maria.

"We used to eat lunch together. I know we've been using that time to study or practice, but we can make time to have lunch together. Let's try for three days a week," said Cooper, her earrings swinging as she spoke.

Jessie nodded her head. "Chuki's right. Let's start with lunch and meet up at the holiday dance on Friday. So let's agree on three days this week."

Julie and Maria looked surprised to hear Jessie and Cooper agree on something—especially something that meant more time. They jumped at the opportunity. Everyone took out their calendars and settled on three days before Home Base was over.

Before leaving, Jessie handed her journal to Mr. Reynolds, with Cooper right behind her. The envelope with the sketches, however, seemed to have a life of its own. It fell out, scattering sheets of paper around Mr.

Reynolds's desk. Quickly, Jessie bent to snatch them up. One floated free. Cooper's hand caught it. The sketch was of her in a practice class in a series of exercises.

"You draw me dancing?" Cooper asked incredulously.

"Sometimes. I'm not that good." Jessie felt the heat of embarrassment.

"Yes, you are," said Cooper.

Mr. Reynolds accepted the sketches. He placed both journals on the desk behind him. "So Miss Williams and Miss Cooper, are you discovering new aspects of one another?"

"Yes, we are, Mr. Reynolds," Jessie replied.

"Oh! I just heard one of the most powerful, positive words one good human being can say regarding another. That word is 'we.' Now that is what I call an outstanding first step toward mutual respect. Make it a good day!"

Outside, the girls exchanged rehearsal and practice schedules for the week. Jessie wanted to make amends. She recalled something Mamatoo had once said: "Any fool can speak a word, few folks can be that word." Jessie had said the word, "we." How could she *be* the word?

"Hey, Chuki, wait a minute. Dad's got a poet and author, Sonia Sanchez, coming to the bookstore Thursday night. You'd like her. She's tough. You want to come and help out?" Jessie stumbled over the words, "Cass will be there. And Joe. Maybe Mom."

From a short distance, Cooper regarded her. Kids milled around them in the crowded hall.

"I've been reading Sonia Sanchez since I was in fourth grade," said Cooper, tossing her book bag over her shoulder. "I don't need nobody's charity. Like you said, it's your family, not mine."

Jessie stood there, feeling like a fool. Hot anger started boiling and bubbling inside of her. Instead of pushing it down, however, Jessie turned it around.

"How would I feel if I were Cooper?" she asked herself. The answer was immediate: "Just like she does."

In math class, Jessie struggled with a problem set. Getting a B required A grades. That was the law of averages. English class was better. She'd read both books and analyzed them. In discussion group, Jessie more than held her own.

The Fours met for lunch, staking out their old table. By the time lunch ended, some of the old camaraderie was back and they were caught up on the details of each other's living treasure. Jessie still felt behind the others, but assured them that Miss Harding would come through, like the star she was.

In Home Base, Jessie got her journal back from Mr. Reynolds. His response took half a page.

Dear Miss Williams,

Growing up isn't the hard part. Growing into yourself is. That process takes a lifetime. Along the way, we make mistakes out of ignorance, fear, and arrogance. Your explosive temper results from all three. Try to be gentle and patient with yourself and your many talents. Maybe you see a lot of yourself in Miss Cooper. Consider that. Make it a good day.

Cooper was reading her journal with the same intensity as Jessie.

After rehearsal, Jessie checked the schedule Cooper had given her. The African Dance Troupe was practicing in the dance theater. During the forty minutes she spent watching and listening to them, Jessie sketched. Cooper had moved up to the second line! Jessie imagined the hours of grueling practice Cooper had put in, dancing the same step a thousand times until she was satisfied.

When the rest of the dance group left the stage, so did Cooper. Jessie swung her book bag over her shoulder. Cooper glanced up at her. Lingering, Jessie waited until the stage was empty. Quickly, she scurried to a seat far on the opposite side of the theater, deep in a corner. The small theater was dark, except for the stage lights.

Cooper came back. Upstage center she placed a fancy straw hat and a black shawl on the floor. Excited, Jessie leaned forward. There was a definite sequence to the dance now. The story of Addie Mae Collins from Birmingham, Alabama, had form and structure. Jessie sketched the dance.

Waking to a glorious morning with joyous gospel music, the dancer dressed for church. Cooper took the straw hat with white flowers and yellow ribbons, and placed it on her head with deliberate care. The music changed. Jessie saw her glide to church, then down the church basement stairs to Sunday school with her friends.

When a bomb exploded, Jessie almost jumped out of her seat, until she realized the sound came from the tape. The sound faded to ambulance sounds and screaming. Cooper threw the hat across the stage. The yellow ribbons flapped in the air. As Cooper leaped and turned, Jessie drew.

The mournful strains of "Sometimes I Feel Like a Motherless Child" filled the theater. Cooper crawled across the stage to the black shawl. Wrapping it around her head and shoulders, she stood. The funeral began.

By the end of the dance, Jessie was wrung dry. As Cooper clutched the straw hat to her chest, the Black National Anthem, "Lift Every Voice and Sing," played. Jessie wiped her eyes. Finally, Cooper collapsed on the stage. In her mind, Jessie heard applause.

"Jessie Williams!" Her name rang through the dark theater.

Jessie leaped out of her skin. Her stomach dropped to her toes and her flight instinct kicked in. Frantic, she grabbed her sketchbook and pencils, stuffed them in the book bag, and jumped up.

"Don't run away. You've been sneaking around and spying on me," Cooper yelled.

Breathing deeply, Jessie willed herself to stay calm, remembering the words "ignorance, fear, and arrogance." Mr. Reynolds had written that anger came from those feelings.

One by one she took the steps down to the stage. And with each step, Jessie repeated, "I will not lose my temper. I will not lose my temper. I will not lose my temper."

She reached the front row. Cooper stood far above her on stage.

"So?" asked the dancer.

Jessie shrugged her shoulders. "So, I sneaked. So, I spied on you. So, you caught me. You knew I was there, I mean here, from the beginning? How?"

"Jess, just because you're dark, doesn't make you invisible. When I dance, I know where I am and where everyone else is," said Cooper, wiping the sweat from her face, neck, and arms with a towel. "So?" she repeated.

"So, what?" One strong bite of her bottom lip reminded Jessie to stay calm.

"What do you think of my dance?" Intelligent hazel eyes bore a hole into the space in front of Jessie.

For seconds Jessie struggled, not sure of whether she could speak from her heart.

"Your dance is great! I think everybody should see it," Jessie replied. Not good enough. She tried again. "Cooper, you've created a story that needs to be seen and heard, and felt."

Cooper frowned. "I didn't create this dance for everybody. Just for me. And for Mr. Stinson, my friend at Evergreen. I recorded his blues song about the bombing for my dance. So, you still haven't told me what *you* think."

Jessie grinned. "You're great. The dance is unbelievable. I'm sorry for sneaking to watch you, but I couldn't stay away. I wanted to see your dance every chance I got. I had to see what it was becoming. It's like watching magic, Cooper. Unique magic!"

Cooper pursed her lips. "Unique magic, huh? Like what you do when you act?"

Something changed between Jessie and Cooper.

Jessie reached her hand up and out.

From the stage, Cooper reached her hand down. Their hands met in a high five.

In the same breath, they grinned and whooped, "Unique magic!"

As soon as Jessie got home, she changed clothes. It was hard to ignore the matching tulip sheets, pillowcases, and sham on her bed. Cass had engineered her payback well. Jessie vowed to change her bed every week. No more tulips! Lugging her books upstairs, she carefully arranged them on the kitchen table.

Thanks to her "Do and die" plan, she had been in good homework shape today. But in barely two weeks, grades would be mailed out. The week after Christmas. Surrounded by sharpened pencils, a dictionary, thesaurus, reams of paper, and notebooks, Jessie hit the books.

She'd forgotten her newest prop! A dash downstairs took care of that. Back at the work table, Jessie perched the clear black-framed glasses on the bridge of her nose. An old sweater, pair of jeans, and her tattered pink bunny rabbit slippers completed her costume. Before Dad came home, she'd have to use some dark makeup to smudge the skin under her eyes. What a smart new strategy, "Look the part of a suffering student."

Mom and Cass rolled their eyes when they saw Jessie, but when Mamatoo came upstairs to visit, she winked. Encouraged, Jessie concentrated, refusing to eat anywhere but at the kitchen table, while hitting the books.

"Now, Jessie, don't you think you have carried this act of yours far enough?" asked Mrs. Williams, holding a bowl of steamed eggplant. "Acting won't produce the B grades your father is demanding."

"But, Mom, you have to admit that Jess is great at it," laughed Cass. "She might pull this one off!"

While the two of them laughed, Jessie fumed. Her temperature rose along with her temper.

Mamatoo took her seat at the dining room table. She selected a wheat roll.

"Daughter, Cass, why are you laughing at Jess?" she asked.

Mrs. Williams set the eggplant dish on the table. "Mother, we're not laughing at her. To Jess, life is a play and she's the lead."

"And my sister will provide the setting, props, makeup,

lights, and the rest of the cast, if she needs to," added Cass.

Waving her butter knife at the two of them, Mamatoo frowned. "Don't you two realize that Jessie moves to a different beat? When the world sings, be it a dirge or a lullaby, Jessie hears her own beat. Most artistic folk are like that. They live slightly out of step with the world around them. So show some compassion here."

Jessie pushed the glasses to the top of her head. With a pencil behind each ear, there wasn't room for much more. Peering over the pile of thick books in front of her, she grinned.

"Thanks, Mamatoo," called Jessie. "I appreciate the support."

Her grandmother called back, "Twenty four hours, seven days a week, Jess."

By the time Mr. Williams came home, the family was asleep. Except for Jessie.

"Hi, Dad. Mom left a plate for you in the oven," she said. "How's the store?"

Mr. Williams hung up his coat. "All those books? How many subjects are you taking, girl? You should be in bed."

"No rest for serious students, Dad. You know that. Pulling good grades at OPA is tough. My teachers are hard," Jessie said.

"I'll pull up a chair and eat here, if you don't mind. Can I move these?"

Jessie reached over. "I'll do it, Dad. My books are in a certain order."

"When did you start wearing glasses?"

Jessie sighed. "Dad, I know this sounds weird, but when I wear clear glasses, I study longer."

A lift of his eyebrows revealed his skepticism. He wasn't stupid, after all. "Well, whatever works, within reason, of course. I am impressed with the amount of attention you are giving to your schoolwork. I hope it shows in your grades."

"Not half as much as I do, Dad. I love OPA. Dad, OPA is one of the first places where I feel like I belong," Jessie said earnestly.

Mr. Williams looked up from his dinner. "I know that you believe that I am harsh with you. But I get scared for you, Jessie. I want you in a safe world, where you have a stable career and future. Acting is a precarious, unstable life with no guarantees."

This was her chance to tell her father how she felt. "Dad, I can't be Cass. I can't look like her or take on her dreams. I'm me, Jessie. I know you love her the most—"

Dad dropped his fork. "What! Look like Cass? You're absolutely beautiful. You're the image of your mother! As for loving Cass more, you're wrong. I understand her better. It's easier for me to talk to her. We—"

Jessie smiled, recalling Mamatoo's words earlier that evening. "You and Cass hear the same beat," she said, finishing her father's sentence.

"I guess we do. But that doesn't lessen my love for you. You're my daughter! You're the child your mother and I never thought we could have." Mr. Williams spoke passionately. "Maybe I have been too hard on you. I love you, Jessy Bessy."

Tears filled Jessie's eyes. It had been years since she'd heard Dad call her that.

"And I love you, Dad."

"Good." He cleared his throat. "You need your rest. Pack up the books and go to bed. And next time, you can leave some of the thicker ones at the library. I'm sure they're heavy—and I'm impressed already. Just stick to the essentials and you'll do well." He paused. "A father's job is to worry. But I have faith in you."

They hugged, and Jessie went off to bed feeling happier than she had in months.

In bed, Jessie opened her journal.

Dear Mr. Reynolds,

This has been a day of surprises. I saw Cooper's special dance. It's done, except for some fine tuning. She knew I was there. We talked. Cooper makes magic, unique magic, when she dances. I told her that. Today I learned that controlling my temper makes me stronger. I learned that I live to a different beat. So does Cooper. And maybe my Dad knows that, too. That's all.

◇◇◇

Tuesday somersaulted by. A nervous lunch meeting of the Fours ended in a decision to meet at Evergreen that afternoon and see what their living treasures wanted to do and if they could be ready by tomorrow, when the Fours' presentation had been scheduled. As she went through her classes, Jessie felt like she was at a swap meet. She handed in her completed assignments and her teachers handed her new ones.

Production crews for *Harriet Tubman* had been assigned weeks ago. Headed by experienced eighth-grade students, lighting, costume, set, and sound crews labored in various rooms in the drama wing. With actors swarming onstage, the play hummed like a living thing.

Soon there would be dress rehearsals. Then on Saturday, January second, opening night—the first OPA performance of *Harriet Tubman*. Publicity had gone out to cities in the East Bay as well as San Francisco and Marin County.

That afternoon, Jessie joined the rest of the Fours on their way to Evergreen. While Maria and Julie strolled ahead, Cooper and Jessie walked in comfor-table silence.

"I've been thinking about something," ventured Jessie.

Cooper nodded.

"Would you be willing to share your dance with us— me and Maria and Julie? And Mr. Stinson? And maybe Mr. Reynolds?" Jessie pushed the words out. "Look, Chuki, I've read every newspaper article written about the bombing. You took a horrible thing that people would rather forget, and made it something remarkable. I'm talking about hope and dignity and history."

"You read about Addie Mae Collins? Why?"

Jessie struggled for an answer. "Because as I watched you choreograph your dance, I needed to know as much as possible so I could understand what you were creating."

Cooper grinned. "That shows respect. Thanks. I'll dance, if you narrate. You know the story. You can tell the story, then I'll dance it."

"Really? I accept! What about helping out at the store on Thursday?"

Cooper stopped. "*Why* do you want me to come?"

Jessie thought hard. Mamatoo's advice seemed best: "When nitty hits gritty, 'fess up fast." They were almost at Evergreen.

"I'd feel better. I took my problems out on you. That was wrong."

"Yeah, it was." Cooper paused to let her words sink in. "But I understand how you felt. I'd like to help out on Thursday."

"One more thing." Jessie was really testing this new ground. "Are you going to change your name again?"

Cooper laughed. "Maybe."

"I'd rather keep calling you Cooper," Jessie said.

"No problem." Cooper tossed off the words lightly.

Inside, the girls first met with their elderly friends individually and then they all met together.

Mr. Stinson began. "Well, Chuki has asked me to perform with her and Jessie for a special project, but that won't be ready for tomorrow. But we know you'd like us to come to school tomorrow. I will be happy to come and perform."

Mrs. Lee continued. "We'd like to make a day of it. My son will help me bring in some of my paintings and slide equipment. I'd like to do a lunchtime showing and leave up the artwork for the afternoon. That way, all of the students interested in art can come."

The Morgan sisters raised their hands. Bertha, the elder, began, "Maria has convinced us that we have lived a life worth sharing."

"So kind of her," smiled Beulah, patting Maria's hand.

"We have agreed to attend your Home Base class tomorrow afternoon and bring mementos from our lives and tell a few stories." Bertha grinned at her sister.

"Not too risqué," they said together.

The group laughed.

Everyone looked at Miss Harding and Jessie.

Jessie started to speak, but Miss Harding stopped her. "My friends, especially Jessie, have persuaded me that a visit to your Home Base class tomorrow would be appropriate. Jessie has some of my scrapbooks. I trust that she will handle the introductions."

"And we want to express our appreciation to you fine young ladies for being so respectful and not pressuring us to make decisions, until we were ready," summarized Mr. Stinson, twanging his guitar.

Happy and relieved laughter filled the room.

◇◇◇

That evening, Jessie studied at the kitchen table, waiting for her father to come home. She had resolved not to miss a night until the holiday break. She knew that she wasn't proving anything anymore, but something good was coming out of staying up long after the rest of the family were asleep. She and Dad were talking more.

A few nights ago, Jessie had even got up the courage to ask him about what Cass had told Cooper at the bookstore.

"Cass said there was a time when you missed her birthday and Thanksgiving. I don't remember that at all, but Cass said I was little."

"Oh, Jess," said her father sadly. "Yes, I did miss your sister's birthday and Thanksgiving one year. It was a bad time at the bookstore. We weren't making any money. I'm afraid I took it out on the whole family. I missed Cass's birthday because I thought the store was more important. Your mother and I had a serious quarrel and I stayed away on Thanksgiving. Fool that I was, I thought I was making a point. I wanted her respect." Mr. Williams chuckled quietly. "Well, your mom straightened me out, Jessie. I won't ever abandon my family again. The bookstore is important to me—to all of us. But, my family comes first."

Mr. Williams looked at his daughter warmly.

"Thanks, Dad," said Jessie.

Mrs. Williams had begun putting up Christmas decorations. A wreath hung on the front door. A garland decorated the fireplace. A host of African-American angels dressed in white lacy dresses stood here and there.

On Sunday morning, after church, the family would get the tree. Then Mr. Williams would fix his special Christmas Tree Pancake Breakfast. They'd spend the day decorating the tree.

In the corner of the living room sat boxes of Kwanzaa symbols and special gifts. Kwanzaa, an African-American holiday celebrating the harvest, began on December 26th and ended on January 1st. There would be seven nights of dinners with friends and relatives, storytelling, and gift-giving. Jessie liked having one holiday run right into the other, but this holiday season was moving nonstop like a roller coaster.

When Jessie got to school on Wednesday, the halls were still empty. She'd never arrived so early. Jessie paused when she rounded the corner to Home Base. Miss Laura Harding was already there.

"Miss Harding!" Jessie greeted her living treasure. "Thanks for being so early."

There was a mischievous twinkle in Miss Harding's eyes. "Good morning, Jessie. I thought I'd walk around a bit and see your special school."

A rich baritone voice from behind startled Jessie.

"I don't believe my eyes! Corrine James? The great Corrine James? Welcome to Oakland Performing Arts Middle School," said Mr. Reynolds, clapping his hands.

"Jessie, this must be your taskmaster, Mr. Reynolds. Thank you," said Miss Harding, the hint of a blush on her cheeks.

"Miss Williams, would you do me the honor of introducing me to this wonderful legend?"

"Miss Harding, I mean, Miss James, I'd like you to meet my drama teacher, Mr. Reynolds. Mr. Reynolds, this is my living treasure, Miss Corrine James, star of stage and screen." With a flourish, Jessie completed the introdutions.

"I can't tell you what an honor it is to meet you, Miss James."

"Thank you again, Mr. Reynolds."

The hall was no longer empty, but Jessie's teacher stood there like a starstruck kid.

"Hey, Mr. Reynolds, we've got class," said Jessie. "Miss James is here for my part of the presentation. I know you thought it would be a woman named 'Miss Harding,' but she doesn't like publicity and I wanted to surprise you."

"Consider me stunned. Miss James, perhaps you would enjoy a tour of the school later. I know you must be busy," Mr. Reynolds rattled on, "but if you would stay, we'd be honored."

"I accept your gracious invitation."

Beaming, Mr. Reynolds offered his arm to Miss Harding and led her into the classroom. A bemused Jessie followed.

Eventually, the rest of the class trooped in. Miss Harding sipped a cup of tea that Mr. Reynolds had dashed off to find for her. She was seated next to Jessie. After roll, Mr. Reynolds began class.

"The Fours have created an unusual project, called

'Living Treasures.' Through their work at Evergreen Residential Home, they have met elderly people of great talent. During the course of this day, they have scheduled appearances for their new friends," he said. "Fours, you have the floor."

Maria waved a bunch of flyers. "Here is the schedule for the entire day. We've posted them all over the school. Everybody take one."

Jessie stood up. "It is my great honor to introduce one of the greatest drama and movie stars of all times, Miss Corrine James. She is the winner of two Tony Awards and an Oscar for Supporting Actress. But most of all she is a great lady. I will pass around three of her personal scrapbooks. Be very careful with them. I present Miss James."

Jessie watched her friend toss off her cape and walk to the front of the room like a star. Today she wore a red silk suit with diamond and pearl earrings and the gold locket pin. The room was hushed. She sat on the stool, commanding the attention of each class member, and spoke eloquently about her life on stage and screen. Twenty minutes later, the room rang with applause and cheers. Almost every hand was up, eager to ask a question.

As the bell rang, Mr. Reynolds swooped toward the star and ushered her out of the classroom. Miss Harding managed to wave at Jessie and throw her a kiss. A warmth spread through Jessie. There was nothing like sweet success.

During the rest of the morning, Jessie caught sight of her teacher and Miss Harding in the center of admiring throngs of students and teachers. Miss Harding looked somewhat overwhelmed, but pleased.

The rest of the day was one triumph after another. The Morgan sisters were a smash! In fact, the students asked them to come back. Maria had to set up an autograph table for them outside the Home Base room.

As for Mrs. Lee, Julie's arrangements with the art department paid off. A small theater had been prepared for the slide presentation. Several of Mrs. Lee's paintings were displayed in the school gallery. The lunch crowd overflowed into the hallway. The head of the art department invited her to return for a series of lectures.

Somehow Cooper had snared the cafeteria and set up a place for Mr. Stinson to play after school. As the music drifted out into the halls, the cafeteria filled. Instead of rushing home or to the library, students found seats on chairs, tables, and even the floor, and stayed to the end. Mr. Stinson sang and played like the pro he was. Jessie spied Miss Harding sitting near the front with Mr. Reynolds.

By the end of the day, an exhausted, proud group of girls headed for home. There was still Cooper's dance to look forward to.

◇◇◇

On Thursday, Jessie crammed in as much computer time as she could during the school day, leaving no room for breaks. By evening she was so exhausted, the last thing she wanted to do was to work in the bookstore, but she had promised. With Joe driving, they picked up Cooper on the way. She was waiting outside of her apartment building, alone. Jessie gazed up. The apartment was dark.

Once at the bookstore, Jessie set up the chairs and the podium in the Author Room. Something looked wrong. There it was. The large framed photograph of Toni Morrison was badly askew. Time was running out! Sonia Sanchez had just arrived.

Knowing how important it was to her father to have everything perfect for an author appearance, Jessie dashed to the back room and hauled a ladder to the spot. She jerked the ladder straight and carefully began to climb the rungs. As she reached to straighten the photograph, the ladder began to totter. There was nothing to hold onto!

"Jessie!" yelled Cooper, sprinting over from the doorway.

The ladder tipped sideways. Cooper somehow grabbed the ladder, but Jessie was falling. Down she tumbled, hitting the floor with a thud.

Cooper was there. "Are you hurt? Don't move, Jess! Just check yourself—legs, arms, back. Real careful, now."

Jessie did. When she tried to move her left arm, the one beneath her, she cried out. The pain was bad. Suddenly, Dad, Cass, and Joe were there.

Margaret agreed to handle the store and the poet. Cass asked Joe to stay behind and help. Mr. Williams carried Jessie to the van. Cooper insisted on coming along to the emergency room.

When Jessie got out of the X-ray room, Mom and Mamatoo were waiting with the rest of the family. Cooper was pale. Cass was paler. Dad paced while Mom wrung her hands. Only Mamatoo remained calm.

"Just a little break. That's all," said Jessie, trying to sound cheerful.

Soon the cast was on and Jessie's arm was in a sling. Before long she was back in the van. The painkiller made her sleepy.

"Jess, tell me why you got up on that ladder! You know I don't allow that," said Mr. Williams, braking for a red light.

"I had to straighten the picture. I wanted everything to be the way you like it, Dad."

"Jessie, your safety comes first," he said.

Mamatoo spoke up. "Perhaps making you happy mattered more to her. Your approval matters more to this child than you realize."

But Jessie was fast asleep. Only her mother saw the stricken expression on Dad's face.

Jessie awoke to find herself tucked in bed, surrounded by her family. Her father stood in the doorway, while her mother fussed around her.

"Are you in pain?" asked Cass.

Jessie shook her head. "Not much. Cooper practically made a swan dive trying to catch me. If it hadn't been for her I'd be in worse shape. She made me lie still. And she kept the ladder from falling on me."

Mamatoo kissed her. "That's what friends are for. Sleep heals, child, so sleep good tonight and tomorrow."

"What about school? I have tests to take! The holiday dance is tomorrow night! The play is in two weeks. Will Mr. Reynolds let me be in it with this?" She looked from one face to another for answers.

"Jessie, pay attention to me." It was Mamatoo, again. "This is short and sweet, but true. Like socks, life sorts itself out. Good night, Jess."

Just as Jessie reached for the light, her father bent over and kissed her on the forehead. "Please don't ever rush on my account and hurt yourself again, Jess. Not for any reason."

"I won't, Dad."

"Good night, Jessy Bessy. I love you."

"Me too, Dad."

During the night, Jessie woke up. Moonlight poured in. When she turned, she felt the cast. With effort, she got her journal and a pencil, and found an empty page.

> Dear Mr. Reynolds,
>
> It's hard to write with a cast. So this will be short. Cooper and I are on the way to being friends. I think that sometimes it is hard for two people with unique magic to be friends, but we found our beat. Wait until you see our special project! Get ready for the best. That's all.

"**M**om! I have to go to school! I'm fine. Please, Mom," begged Jessie, "I promise to be careful. The doctor said I could go to school."

Mrs. Williams looked at her husband. "Honey, what do you think?"

"Do you want to go because you want to please me?" he asked.

Jessie shook her head. "No, Dad. I want to go because I have important things to do."

"Then find something warm to wear and go to school,"

he said, attempting to sound stern. "Don't injure anyone with that cast."

Jessie planted a big kiss on his cheek, "Dad, you're the best!"

"I needed to hear that. Thank you, Jess."

Getting through the day was much easier than Jessie had imagined. Jamar met her at the end of each class and carried her book bag. He brought lunch to her table, and generally hung around. Maria and Julie were never far behind. Jessie felt as if she were being followed by a throng of anxious mothers. At least Cooper gave her room to breathe.

Jessie refused her teachers' offers to let her make up work at a later time. For the first time since fourth grade and Mrs. Grant, she was handling both schoolwork and acting. Studying was becoming a habit she intended to keep. Maybe those glasses did help!

The stage was crowded for the after-school rehearsal of *Harriet Tubman*. Mr. Reynolds hadn't said anything, yet. Jessie prayed that he would let her stay in the play. She knew she could carry her part.

"Jess, I'm going to put your book bag here. I'll walk you to the bus after rehearsal," said Jamar.

"Thanks. Do you think I'll get to stay in the play?" Jessie asked Jamar candidly.

But it was Mr. Reynolds who answered. "I have no intention of losing your talent. Get on stage, the chorus needs you!"

When Jessie and Jamar left school, Mamatoo was waiting in her car.

"Thought you might appreciate a ride. Jamar, thank you for taking such good care of my granddaughter. Can I offer you a lift?" she asked, opening the car door.

"No, Ma'am, but thank you. Be careful, Jessie," he said. "Do you think you'll make it to the dance?"

"I'll try, but I can't promise."

"I'll call and see how you are. Bye, Jessie."

Jessie's eyes followed Jamar as he walked away. So did Mamatoo's.

Normally Mamatoo drove like a fire truck going to a twelve alarm blaze, but not this foggy Friday afternoon. She even had a pillow for Jessie to rest the cast on. Jessie was grateful. It had been an exhausting day.

"Jessie, my dear, in one short semester at OPA, so much has happened to you. Not only the arm. More vital parts of you have broken open to let in the light. Remember that talk we had before the meeting with Mrs. Grant?"

Jessie nodded. "Yes. I didn't have any answers."

"And now?"

"Mrs. Grant was wrong. I know that now," said Jessie.

"Exactly what I've been praying to hear you say. You look so tired, Jessie. How about taking a long nap in my modest domicile before deciding about the dance tonight?"

"That sounds good."

In the end, going to the dance proved to be too much. When Jamar called, Jessie apologized for not going.

"Nonsense," replied Jamar. "But I won't dance with anyone but you."

"Nonsense," retorted Jessie. They quibbled until Jessie agreed he could sit out one dance in her honor.

The phone rang again.

Jessie picked it up. "Hello?"

"Jessie, this is Miss Harding. I heard about your arm. Are you all right?"

"Thanks for calling, Miss Harding. I'll be fine." Jessie went on. "The whole school is still talking about you," she said. "And, you know my friend who likes Judith Jamison? Do you think you could get an autograph for her for me? She's the one who tried to catch me when I fell off the ladder and broke my arm."

"That's the very least I can do. We'll talk soon over a cup of my special tea," promised Miss Harding. "And thank you, Jessie, for a second chance at life. I am considering a return to the stage."

Jessie was flabbergasted. All she could think to say was, "I hope so. Thanks for calling."

The week flew by. Late Saturday night, she finished her narrative for Cooper's dance, tapping the keys at the computer. Now she had to commit it to memory.

Sunday, after Dad's Christmas Tree Pancake Breakfast, she called Cooper. The theater would be free on Wednesday afternoon, December 23rd, the last day before break.

They divided up the list of people to invite. It was too short. After Jessie hung up the phone, she scribbled down a few more names.

"Jess, after we decorate the tree, I want to wash your hair and set it," said Mrs. Williams.

"Can we do it later? I have some work to do, Mom."

Mrs. Williams marveled at this new daughter of hers.

By Tuesday night, telephone invitations to Cooper's dance were completed, and Jessie wrapped her Christmas gifts. The Williams family had a tradition of keeping gift-giving very inexpensive and simple. She and Cass had gone shopping together, buying their presents from the vendors on Telegraph Avenue in Berkeley.

◇◇◇

Butterflies fluttered in Jessie's stomach from the moment she opened her eyes on Wednesday morning. She had taken some big risks for the dance performance. Cooper would either kill her or thank her. The stakes were high, but worth it.

Jessie's trip to the dance theater was no secret this time. She entered the theater with Maria and Julie. She had dressed in black: sweater, pants, and shoes. In her book bag was a long red, black, and green scarf—the colors of liberation—which Mamatoo had lent her. Cooper would be surprised. The guests from Evergreen Residential Home were already seated. Mr. Reynolds was chatting with Miss Harding. Her Home Base class, her family, and Joe were seated behind Mr. Williams.

Jessie found Cooper in the wings.

"I'll hook your tape up to the sound system. Jamar has a chair and a mike for Mr. Stinson. He's setting it up now. Where are the lights? I'll throw a floodlight on you," said Jessie. "Relax, all you have to do is dance."

"Where did you learn to do lights and sound?" asked Cooper.

Jessie laughed. "When you meet Mamatoo, my grandmother, you'll understand. If you work in her theater, you learn how to do everything."

"I am so nervous," admitted Cooper, biting her nails.

"Let's go over the plan. I go onstage and introduce Mr. Stinson. He comes up. While I narrate, he plays just the music to his song, 'Birmingham Sunday School Blues.' I finish. Mr. Stinson sings the song. You come on. The tape starts. You dance. Right?"

Cooper hopped up and down, trying to loosen up. "Jess, what if I forget?"

"Your own choreography? Come on, Cooper, we make magic!"

"That's right! We do!" Cooper looked a little more relaxed.

"Now, don't come out, or look out, until Mr. Stinson stops singing. Break a leg," teased Jessie. "Sorry, that's for actors, not dancers!"

"I like your scarf," Cooper said. "It's perfect. Thanks, Jessie."

Crossing the fingers of her right hand, Jessie hoped that Cooper would feel the same way after the performance was over.

A chair and low microphone were downstage right. Jamar had taken care of everything, and Mr. Stinson was ready and waiting. Jess adjusted the floodlight and took her seat on stage. She looked around. It was time to begin. Following a nod from Jessie, Mr. Stinson began to play.

The back theater doors opened quietly and a lone woman came in. She sat in a middle row on the end. A man came in and sat across the aisle from her. Silently students filed in until the theater was packed. Kids lined up in the back and sat in the aisles. Jessie let the blues music create the mood. Mr. Stinson finished his song and then began again to accompany Jessie's narration.

When she finished telling the tragic story, Mr. Stinson sang the unforgettable story of the four girls murdered on an Alabama Sunday morning. The theater was absolutely still. As the last strains of the guitar faded away, Cooper stood in the floodlight. Jessie prayed that Cooper wouldn't panic when she saw a theater packed with unexpected guests. Jamar immediately started the tape. Cooper began to dance.

Time stopped while Cooper danced. She performed each step flawlessly. Cooper seemed to dance as if she were the only person in the theater. When Cooper put on the straw hat, Jessie cried. And when Cooper marched to the Black National Anthem, Jessie almost joined her! The performance ended. The audience sat still.

To Jessie's surprise, Cooper stood up, faced the audience, and spoke.

"My name is Addie Mae Cooper. Addie Mae Collins is my relative. We are blood kin. I dedicate this dance to her, and to the other three murdered children and their families."

The applause started and built. Kids were clapping and yelling! Cooper beckoned to Jessie and Mr. Stinson. They joined her centerstage.

"Jess," whispered Cooper, out of the corner of her mouth. "That's my mother and father out there."

"Yes. I invited them."

"And all these kids?" she asked.

Jessie shrugged one shoulder, "You must have a good reputation."

"How'd you get my parents here?"

"I told them to come and see you make magic."

"Thank you, Jessie."

"You owe me one," whispered Jessie. "Hey, I bet we'll get an A from Mr. Reynolds, Cooper."

Cooper whispered back, "We'd better get an A! And call me Addie Mae, from now on." She took hold of Jessie's hand.

Jessie grinned from ear to ear. Light flooded the stage. The applause continued. Mr. Reynolds, Miss Harding,

Maria, Julie, and Jamar looked so proud. Sitting next to them waving her arms was Mamatoo!

Jessie stared down at her hand in Addie Mae's. Different colors. One dark, the other fair. But they shared something stronger—dreams and the unique magic to make them come true.

Right then and there, Jessie knew that everything was going to work out. She'd make the grades and stay at OPA. *Harriet Tubman* would be a hit. The "Living Treasures" project would grow and grow. Eventually, Dad would understand her because he loved her.

In the meantime she would count on Mamatoo's wise words—"Like socks, life sorts itself out."

About the Author

Candy Dawson Boyd's first book, *Circle of Gold,* was selected as a Coretta Scott King Award Honor Book. Her book *Charlie Pippin* (Puffin) was both an IRA-CBC Children's Choice Book and an ALA Notable Book. She lives in San Pablo, California.